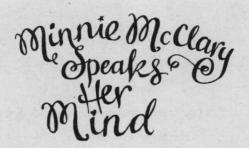

Also by Valerie Hobbs

Tender
The Last Best Days of Summer
Sonny's War
Letting Go of Bobby James, or How I Found My Self of Steam
Anything but Ordinary
Defiance
Sheep

Minnie McClary Speaks Her Mind

Valerie Hobbs

SCHOLASTIC INC.

ISBN 978-0-545-63146-4

12 11 10 9 8 7 6 5 4 3   13 14 15 16 17 18/0

Printed in the U.S.A.   40

First Scholastic printing, September 2013

Designed by Roberta Pressel

For Myrna, a wise teacher and dear friend

I0:02. Room 2, Mojave Middle School, Home of the Mustangs.

Minnie McClary, row one, seat four, nervously watched the clock. If a teacher did not show up in exactly three minutes, Room 2 was going to explode. It had happened yesterday, and the day before that, and it was sure to happen again.

Some little thing would set it off, a belch or a fart, a spitwad would fly. Kids would wriggle in their seats. One boy would leave his desk, then another. They would prowl the room like dogs sniffing for trouble, or do some dopey thing to make everybody nervous, like standing on the teacher's desk.

Minnie was trying not to worry about what would happen today. It was not her job to keep order. Like the rest of the class, she was only a kid. Unlike them, she was the *new* kid. She didn't know where she fit in yet, or if she ever would.

She bit her lip and waited.

10:03. Feet shuffled, backpacks unzipped, forbidden cell phones appeared. Alicia, who always sighed dramatically, sighed dramatically. The boy who had allergies and never blew his nose began his nervous sniffle. Somebody hummed the theme from *Jaws*. Derek's fingers drummed the desk.

Minnie tried to think about things outside this classroom, like the blank canvas in art class that was supposed to turn into a self-portrait. Her brother, Dylan, who had stopped being nice the minute he turned thirteen. Her uncle Bill, who was building a helicopter in the basement.

She tried not to think about her mom and dad arguing about Uncle Bill, but one thought led to the next, and then she was worrying. Minnie worried too much, her mother said. She should be having fun, like a normal eleven-year-old girl.

10:04. Amira, the girl across from Minnie, turned to her with dark, troubled eyes. She seemed to be thinking what Minnie was thinking: what if *nobody* came? In the three weeks since school began, their class had had five different subs. Only one of them, the principal's wife, stayed longer than two days. She had gone on and on about the beauty of verb phrases, and then went home and had a baby.

Mr. Delgado came next. He yelled so loud the windows rattled.

Miss Valentine, number three, had laryngitis and couldn't talk at all.

Mr. Spinks, a retired engineer, taught them how to make stealth planes out of notebook paper. He didn't know what a verb phrase was.

And now their language arts class had fallen apart.

10:05. "Ow!" yelled Carl. He leaped from his desk, rubbing the back of his head. "Who did that?" He dived on Jorge and knocked him to the floor. Two of the girls and all of the boys, except for Todd Ingram, whose mother was the school board president, flocked to the back of the room.

Todd sat quietly and drew. Theresa the goth girl opened a book and began to read. Amira bowed her head. A trash can went clattering across the floor. Kids yelled and whooped and jumped around Carl and Jorge, who were scuffling on the floor.

Minnie counted to ten. Twice. She looked at the door through which no one was coming. She checked the clock:

10:06. Her face felt hot and her ears itched. She could not keep her feet still. Without thinking, without really knowing what she was doing, Minnie jumped up out of her seat and, with her fists clenched, shouted "Stop!" as loud as her voice would go. "Stop it!"

And something extraordinary happened. As if Minnie had cast a spell, every kid in the room did exactly what she said. They stopped what they were doing and froze in place. Now they were all staring at her, at Minnie the new girl, the very short, hardly noticeable new girl in the first row. Even Amira, the girl who might have been a friend, stared at her in horror, as if Minnie had sprouted horns.

Even Minnie seemed to be staring at Minnie. She could not believe what she had done, or that the floor would not open and let her drop through.

10:07. The doorway filled with the huge body of their principal, Mr. Butovsky, wearing his navy blue suit and a red tie knotted beneath his chins. "Back to your seats!" he bellowed. Kids scurried to their desks, quick as lizards. Minnie slid into her seat, her heart ticking like a clock gone haywire.

Mr. Butovsky had been their sub for two days. He had read to them out of a book called *Crime and Punishment*.

For a while the class had been patient. But the words were huge and the sentences went on forever. "So he kept torturing himself," Mr. Butovsky had read, looking down over his three chins and through the reading glasses balanced on the end of his nose, "tormenting himself with these questions, and he seemed even to derive some pleasure from it."

No one could understand why the principal had chosen to read them the crime book. Yes, they had been bad. Yes, they had thrown spitwads and played games on the phones they weren't supposed to bring to class. But they didn't murder any little old ladies like the guy in the book did.

They had listened a while longer to find out what their punishment would be. Maybe this *was* their punishment! One by one they had all given up on the crime book, even Minnie, who always did everything right.

But Mr. Butovsky was upbeat today and all of his chins were smiling. "I have some very good news, children," he said, righting the trash can. "We have found you a teacher."

Nobody said a word. Room 2, fourth-period language arts, was wary of new teachers who blew in and out like the wind across the desert.

"Her name is Miss Marks and she'll be starting to-morrow," he said. "You will have her for the rest of the year."

"The *whole* year?" said Alicia, who was pretty and brave and always spoke up.

"The whole year," said Mr. Butovsky. "Now let's get to work, shall we?" He opened *Crime and Punishment* to the page he had marked. Eyes glazed over. Jorge laid his head on his desk. Carl used his backpack as a pillow. Amira sat without seeming to breathe, as patient as stone.

Minnie tried, really tried, to listen, but all she could think about, the *only* thing she could think about, was what she had done. The enormity of the thing. How she had jumped right up out of her seat and yelled at the top of her lungs. She still couldn't believe that she'd done it. Her face tingled with shame. Her whole body felt hot and sticky. It was *wrong*. It was wronger than wrong: it was embarrassing, and she would never live it down.

She sat with her hands clenched together, her own shrill voice still ringing in her ears.

Mr. Butovsky looked up from the book, squinting at the window. "Will somebody please lower that blind?" he said. Nobody moved. Then Carl, from the very last seat in the very last row, in his nastiest, nasally voice, said, "Let Miss Goody-Goody do it."

Every face turned toward Minnie.

Derek and Carl did a fist bump. "Dude!" said Derek.

Somebody snickered, then somebody else.

Minnie stopped breathing. She blinked and blinked to hold back her tears, but they leaked out all the same, rolling over her cheeks and off her chin as Amira, wearing her black head scarf, got up and with her perfect dancer's posture went to the window and lowered the blind, and Minnie waited to die.

MINNIE TOOK TWO CANS OF PEPSI OUT OF THE
FRIDGE AND OPENED THE DOOR TO THE BASEMENT.
A stew of smells—grease, laundry detergent, orange peels,
musty sheets, and dirty socks—rose up to greet her. She
started down the stairs.

Her uncle Bill was asleep on his Salvation Army couch,
curled up with his arms around his chest. His gray T-shirt
was the one he'd worn yesterday, and the day before that.
It was stained with grease and something that looked
like blood but was probably catsup. He was going to shave
"someday," he said, but that day didn't seem to be coming. His face was beginning to look mangy, like the back
end of Tuffy, the neighbor's dog.

Minnie was beginning to think she would never get
her "old" uncle back. The one who laughed harder at kid
movies than she did. The one who taught her magic tricks
and sang off-key on purpose. In church! The uncle who
was more fun than anybody she ever knew.

Minnie ducked under a helicopter blade, stepped over

a box of metal parts, and poked her uncle's shoulder. "Uncle Bill!"

"Mmmmph," he said, opening an eye.

"I brought you a Pepsi." He didn't move.

She pushed his shoulder again. This time, he opened both eyes and sat straight up, his eyes wide and wild. *"What? What happened?"*

"Pepsi."

He frowned and ran a hand over his crew cut. In the dim light, his deep-set eyes were a muddy green, his skin pale and ghostly. "Oh," he said, coming back from wherever he'd been. "Thanks, Minnie."

Minnie set the drinks on the floor next to her uncle's prosthetic leg. She sat down beside him. "I did a jerky thing today," she said.

With his arms still crossed, her uncle scratched his armpits. "How jerky?"

"Real jerky," she said. "Stupid jerky." Then she told him what happened in language arts class.

Her uncle nodded thoughtfully, or else he was falling back to sleep. "Uh-huh."

"I don't know why I did it!" she cried. "I've never done a thing like that in my whole life! It was horrible!"

"Horrible." He rubbed his red-rimmed eyes.

"It felt like . . . like . . ." She couldn't come up with a word bad enough, a metaphor right enough. Except for "hell," which she wasn't supposed to say.

Her uncle got a rare twinkle in his green eyes. "It felt good, didn't it?"

"Huh?"

"It felt good," he said, and shrugged.

For a minute, Minnie said nothing. She just stared at her uncle, whose eyes had lost their muddy look. Was he teasing her? How could what she had done feel good?

Well, it couldn't. He was wrong, dead wrong. What she had felt wasn't good, it was awful.

Or was it? The awful came *after*, didn't it? *After* she'd done the horrible thing. What she felt like while it was happening was, yeah, kind of good. As if, for once, she, shrimpy Minnie McClary, was bigger than herself, almost huge.

But after, *after* was horrible. Not worth it. Definitely not worth it. For the rest of the year, she would be still. As silent and still as Amira.

Minnie's uncle smacked her thigh and stood. He switched on the fans her mother had bought at Target, but all they did was push the hot air around. "I'm going to get some work done on the chopper today," he said, hopping over to his toolbox. "You can help, if you want."

His camouflage pants were faded and torn. He'd worn them or his one other pair for two months now, ever since returning from Iraq. But it didn't seem to matter to him how he looked. If he wasn't down here, he was at the dump scavenging for parts or going wherever he went late at night when nobody was around. His clothes always smelled like smoke.

When Minnie warned him that he was going to die of lung cancer if he didn't quit smoking, he had looked at her for a long time. He didn't care. He didn't say it, but it was there in his eyes, along with all the other things he never talked about.

THE HELICOPTER LOOKED LIKE A GIANT INSECT CROUCHED IN THE MIDDLE OF THE CEMENT FLOOR. It wasn't as big as a real Apache AH-64, her uncle said. He'd need a barn to build one of those. But it was huge and took up most of the basement. Squished against the back wall was a worn-out, ugly brown couch, a metal locker, books about aircraft, his laptop on a wooden crate, and boxes of metal parts.

Stacked against the facing wall were all the cardboard boxes bulging with stuff from the family's big, old house in Pasadena. They were "downsizing," her mother said.

This was part of the reason that Uncle Bill didn't have a bedroom. The other part was that he wanted to live in the basement, where he didn't have to talk to anybody but the people who wanted to talk to him: Minnie, her mother, and once in a while, Minnie's brother, Dylan.

Upstairs, the front door slammed. Her uncle jumped, dropping his screwdriver.

"It's okay," said Minnie. "It's just my dad."

Her uncle's hands shook. Not because of Minnie's father, but because of the war. The only time they didn't shake was when he slept.

He picked up his screwdriver. Reaching into his pocket, he took out a handful of screws. He stared at them so long that Minnie got nervous.

"We're getting a new teacher," she said to get his mind off the screws. "Her name is Miss Marks."

Her uncle looked up. His eyes focused. He smiled. "Another substitute?"

"For the rest of the year, Mr. Butovsky said."

Her uncle tossed his screwdriver into the toolbox. "What happened to the teacher you were supposed to have?"

Minnie shrugged. "I don't know. Maybe he got fired."

"Or she," her uncle said.

Minnie's father had gotten fired, which was why they were "downsizing." He'd been fired for blowing a whistle. Not a real, actual whistle. It had something to do with telling on his boss, which wasn't exactly tattling but sounded like tattling.

When Minnie's mother tried to explain it to Minnie and Dylan, she only confused them more. "Your dad got punished for doing the right thing," she said. Their father didn't want to talk about it.

When Minnie asked her mother why grownups got away with not talking about stuff when kids always had to, her mother said she didn't feel like talking about it.

And she wasn't even kidding!

"I hope Miss Marks is nice," said Minnie wistfully. She had always liked language arts. After art—which was ruined now because of the self-portrait thing—language arts had been her favorite subject. "I hope she's pretty."

Her uncle gave her a warning look. "Minnie . . ."

Minnie grinned. "Don't worry, I won't try to fix you up."

"Again," said her uncle. "You won't try to fix me up *again*."

"I know, I know." She sighed. "It didn't work out last time."

He gave her nose a poke. "You tricked me."

Well, it was true, sort of. It was true that Minnie had talked her uncle into coming upstairs for dinner, which he almost never did. And it was true that she had talked her mother into inviting Beth Keller, who lived with Tuffy the terrier next door.

But it wasn't true that she had played a mean trick. Minnie had meant to do a good thing for her uncle *and* for Miss Keller, who hadn't had a date, she'd said, in seven years.

All through the dinner, her uncle hadn't said one word, while Miss Keller went on and on about updating her bedroom to make it more *inviting*.

Minnie's uncle wouldn't speak to Minnie for two whole days, which was awful.

Just then the basement door opened and her father's voice boomed. "Minnie? You down there?"

"Yes."

"Where's your brother?"

"I don't know."

"Come up here and do your homework."

The door shut with a solid sound.

Minnie sighed. "I've gotta go." Halfway up the steps, she turned around. She knew what her uncle would say, but she had to ask anyway. "We're having pizza for dinner. Are you coming up?"

"Not tonight," he said.

"Okay. I'll bring you some."

Her uncle frowned. "You don't have to wait on me, Minnie."

It was true, she didn't have to. But what would he do if she didn't? Starve to death?

No, he wouldn't starve. Minnie had watched him leave the house late one night when reading *Speak* had kept her awake. Twenty minutes later, he was back. Sitting on the front steps with his fake leg stuck out, he ate something wrapped in yellow paper. When he was finished, he stuffed the paper in his pocket and lit a cigarette.

While Minnie fought to keep her eyes open, he just sat on the steps blowing smoke into a dark, starless sky. Then he got up and wandered off in another direction, his hands stuffed into his pockets and his head down.

Minnie's father pinned her with one of his looks. "I don't want you hanging around down there all day," he said, pulling loose the knot in his tie.

Minnie closed the basement door. "I'm not hanging around down there all day," she said. "I just got home from school."

"Did you do your homework?"

"I just got home from school!"

Her father raised his eyebrows. "Excuse me?"

What had gotten into her? She never talked back to

her father. Had something come loose fourth period when she'd yelled at the class? "I'm sorry," she said.

"That's better. Where's your brother? He should be home by now." He popped his can of Diet Pepsi, frowning at the brown foam that bubbled over his fingers.

"He's probably at Eric's or Nathan's," said Minnie. Unlike her, Dylan had friends. He made them as smoothly as the deals he made with Minnie and conveniently forgot to keep.

Her father rolled up his sleeves and pulled off his tie. "How about fixing us a snack?" he said. "I'm going to wash the car."

Minnie took out some cheese and a box of crackers. She cut the cheese into perfectly even slices and set them on a plate.

Dylan came banging through the door. He dumped his backpack on the table. "What's gotten into *him*?"

"Dad?"

"Who else?" He grabbed a slice of cheese and stuffed it into his mouth.

"Hey!" she said.

He tried to snatch another slice of cheese and Minnie slapped his hand.

"Man!" her brother said. "A guy can't get a break around here!"

Minnie gave him the slice he'd touched with his filthy fingers. "Did he tell you to do your homework?"

"Yeah! What's up with that?"

Minnie sighed.

Her father was changing the rules. In Pasadena, where he had been a lawyer, he always worked overtime. Now he taught at Mojave Community College and was home a lot. Minnie and Dylan had always done their homework after dinner. Now he wanted them to do it the minute they got home.

"You have to talk to him," said Dylan.

"Why me?" said Minnie.

"Because," said Dylan.

"That's not an answer!" said Minnie to the back of Dylan's T-shirt.

Minnie called Becky, one of her two best friends in Pasadena. They talked until Minnie's father said she was tying up the phone. Becky had her own pink cell phone, Katya would be getting an iPhone for her birthday, Minnie would be using the family phone forever.

At a quarter to six, her mother came home with the

pizza. She handed the boxes to Minnie and hung her purse on a chair. She had gotten a short haircut to start her new job. It made her look more "professional," she said. But Minnie had liked it better before, long and wavy or caught up in a ponytail.

She liked all things the way they were before. Everything felt fake now, as if they were actors in a reality show.

"Ask your uncle Bill if he wants to have some pizza with us," her mother said.

Minnie's father rolled his eyes. "Why do you insist on doing that?"

"What?" her mother said. But she knew. They all knew.

"He doesn't want to come up," said Minnie. "I already asked him."

"See?" said her father.

"He's a weirdo," said Dylan, snatching a slice of pizza before Minnie could stop him.

"Watch your language," said their mother.

"Well, he is!" said Dylan. "He lives down there like a rat. He's building a stupid attack helicopter! In the basement!"

Their mother slammed the table. "That's enough!"

Minnie was shocked. Her mother was losing it. They all sat down without another word.

Her mother bowed her head and held out her hands. After Dylan's nasty remark about Uncle Bill, Minnie didn't want to take his hand, but it was the way they said grace, and so she had to.

Her father said their usual grace like one long word, "GodisgreatGodisgoodandwethankHimforthisfood-Amen."

"God wouldn't put anchovies on the pizza," said Dylan. "Yuck!"

"The other one's for you and your sister," said their mother. "Plain old cheese."

They chewed in silence. *If this were a reality show,* thought Minnie, *this was the boring part they would cut.*

"So!" said Minnie's mother. "I've got some good news. I'm getting the bonus!" She held up her hand for a high five.

"That's great, Mom," said Minnie, slapping her mother's hand. At first, her mother had been afraid that she couldn't sell cars, but she was great at it.

"Anybody else got good news?" said her mom. Back to her old self, she smiled across the table at Minnie's father.

The bald spot on her father's head had grown from nickel-size to half-dollar-size. "Are you sure you're getting a bonus?"

"Sure I'm sure," her mother said.

She turned to Minnie's brother. "How about you, Dylan? What's the good news?"

"Eric said I could buy his brother's old dirt bike."

"With what?" their father grumbled.

"Minnie?" said her mother, like the cheerleader she had been in high school a hundred years ago.

"We're getting a new language arts teacher," said Minnie. "For the whole year."

"Great!" said her mother. "That's great news."

"She'll probably leave like all the others," said her father.

"Mr. Gloom and Doom," her mother said.

Minnie wanted to stick up for her dad. He wasn't always Mr. Gloom and Doom. He used to be really funny, like when he did the chickie chickie duck duck dance and made them laugh so hard they couldn't breathe.

Everybody seemed to be changing. Her father had turned into a grouch, her brother was a jerk, her mother was slapping tables, Uncle Bill was more of a hermit than ever, and she herself was screeching in class like she'd lost her marbles.

They weren't just downsizing, they were going downhill. Fast.

THE BUZZ BEGAN AFTER FIRST PERIOD AND HAD ALREADY REACHED A FEVER PITCH. Rumors flew through the hall like Jell-O in a food fight.

Did you see her? Can you believe what she has on?

I bet she's not a real teacher!

I had her for second period, and guess what she did? A tap dance!

I had her for first period. Her eyes are two different colors! She's got a nose ring!

A tongue stud!

A tattoo!

You lie!

9:56. Minnie hurried down the hall to Room 2. Stopping just short of the open doorway, she peered into the room.

A girl wearing jeans and a green T-shirt was sitting on the front of the teacher's desk. Her yellow hair was as short as Minnie's uncle Bill's and fuzzy as a duckling's.

Seven studs curved up her left ear. She had a small, pointy nose, a mole on her cheek, and—

She looked toward the door and Minnie ducked away.

Amira came up behind Minnie. "Is the new teacher in there?" she whispered.

"I don't know," Minnie whispered back. "She doesn't look like a teacher."

She let Amira lead the way in.

"Hi!" said the girl on the desk.

"Hello," said Amira in her soft voice, sliding gracefully into her seat.

Minnie tried to smile, but she was nervous and her smile wouldn't work when she was nervous.

There were six other kids in the room and all of them were quiet. The new teacher, if that was what she was, had caught them all off guard. She looked like a teenager. They didn't seem to know what to make of her. Minnie didn't either.

For one thing, she had never seen a teacher wearing jeans, not even at Target, where everybody shopped, even the teachers. But the other rumors were probably just rumors. Both her eyes were a bright, clear blue. Her nose was ringless, and if she had a stud in her tongue, it was hard to tell.

Minnie waited to see if she would do a tap dance.

The rest of the kids came in a herd, but not the usual noisy herd. They went to their desks meekly, like sheep.

"Hi!" said the girl to each of them.

When they were all seated, she went to the board and scrawled her name: Lindsay Marks. Both names. Not Ms. Marks, not even Miss Marks, but her whole real name. Under that she wrote her e-mail address. "In case you have to miss class and need to know what your homework is," she said. "Or if you, you know, just need to talk."

Talk? To a teacher?

Carl's hand shot up. "I need to talk!" he said.

Miss Marks smiled. "Talk," she said. "But first, I need to know your name."

"Carl Youzney," said Carl. "How old are you anyway?"

A tinge of pink lit up Miss Marks's cheeks. "Old enough to be your teacher," she said. "I'm twenty-four. And everything else you need to know about me is here in this letter." She picked up a stack of paper and slid off the desk. "There's one for each of you."

She went to the first row, counted heads, and gave the girl in the first seat six letters.

"Your assignment for tonight is to write a letter back to me," she said, moving from row to row, "telling me all about yourself."

Minnie's heart capsized. She watched the new teacher going from row to row. The fluorescent lights made her yellow hair gleam. *All about yourself?* This was as bad as the art assignment, *worse*.

What did "all about yourself" mean? Minnie wouldn't know where to begin, or if she wanted to begin at all. There were things she didn't tell anybody, not even Uncle Bill. Like the fact that she wore a bra she didn't need, and that her jeans came from the Target kids' department. The jeans looked exactly the same, her mother said, but they didn't. They looked new, and . . . different. It was just so *obvious*.

She glanced down at Miss Marks's letter. Who was this teacher who wanted to know all about her students? What kind of a teacher was she?

"I see that some of you have started reading, but you know what?" said Miss Marks. "I'd rather you read my letter at home. It might even give you some ideas about what to write back to me."

She waited while the kids reluctantly folded their letters or stuffed them into their backpacks.

"I've got something else for you," she said. Opening a box by the side of the desk, Miss Marks took out a pile of spiral notebooks. "Journals."

A couple of kids groaned. Miss Marks smiled. "Ah, but these are not your ordinary journals," she said. "These are called Inquiry Journals. Could someone help me pass them out?"

Minnie's heart squeezed up like a prune. *Don't let Carl say the goody-goody thing, please don't let him.*

Todd raised his hand and Miss Marks set a stack of notebooks on his desk. "No fighting over colors," she said to the class. "Please take the one you're given."

No one listened. Everybody wanted red or blue, nobody would take orange or yellow. Only Theresa took black.

With the remaining notebooks in her hands, Miss Marks scanned the room. Her gaze rested on Minnie. "Would you like to distribute the rest of these?" she said.

Minnie froze. She couldn't move a finger or even an eyelid. *Please don't let him say anything, please!*

"No?" said Miss Marks. She looked at Thomas, the boy in front of Minnie who always picked his nose and wiped it under his desk. "How about you?"

Thomas stood and began passing out the notebooks.

To all the boys and girls in my fourth-period language arts class:

My name is Lindsay Marks. I was born in San Francisco, California, at 8 a.m. on July 13, 1988. My mother said the sun was smiling on that day, but that I was not. I have two older sisters, both married, and a younger brother who is serving with the armed forces in Afghanistan. I love my country, but I hate war.

I despise bigotry, greed, racism, sexism, and okra no matter how it's cooked.

I love cats, dogs, whales, libraries, asparagus, chocolate ice cream, country music, Jane Austen, and lots of other things.

I have always loved to read. The first book I ever owned was called *The Poky Little Puppy*, which I read and read until both covers came off. I am terrible at most sports and never got picked for teams, but I can tap-dance, toss a pizza crust, and stand on my head. (Not all at once.)

I have a white cat with blue eyes named Ellen, who

thinks she has to sleep on my head. Ellen is an honest cat (I think) and I am a plainspoken honest person. You can count on me to tell you the truth.

I graduated from the University of California at Berkeley with a degree in English, and this is my first full-time teaching job. I am so excited that I can't stop smiling about it. All last year I was a substitute teacher in San Francisco, going from school to school and class to class, never getting the chance to really know the students. I see this year as my chance to build a great learning community with all of you.

I believe that someday we will have world peace, a woman president, cars that run on water, free health care for all, and schools as beautiful as churches.

Above all, I believe in the power of words.

Your teacher,
Lindsay Marks

Minnie read Miss Marks's letter three times. The first time she read breathlessly, shocked that a teacher would share so many personal things about herself. Was this what she expected from them? From *her*? Minnie got dizzy just thinking about it.

She called Becky for advice. Becky said to make things up, that Minnie's teacher would never know the difference. Minnie laughed, but really, how fair would it be to lie to a teacher who promised never to lie to you?

The next time Minnie read the letter, she read more slowly, pondering every detail: the soldier brother, Ellen the cat, whales, her friend Jane Austen. She was surprised all over again, this time because she, Minnie McClary, had so many things in common with Miss Marks. How could she not despise war when it took away her uncle's leg and made him feel like living in a basement? She, too, despised okra and loved asparagus. She, too, loved *The Poky Little Puppy*, her first real book.

The third reading made her feel like one of Miss Marks's personal friends. She began to love Miss Marks.

And then she began her letter.

Dear Miss Marks,
    My name is Marin Elizabeth McClary. I was born on December 25, 2000, which means I only get half the presents everybody else gets.

She scribbled out that sentence and crumpled the paper. Greed was one of the things Miss Marks despised.

She began again.

Dear Miss Marks,
   My name is Marin Elizabeth McClary, and I was born on December 25, 2000, which is Christmas Day.

Duh! She crumpled that letter as well.

She began four more letters with dumb first sentences and now her desk was covered with wasted paper.

It was good Miss Marks didn't say anything about paper wasters.

Minnie always did her homework, but she could not do this. Even if she could get as far as a second sentence, she didn't know what would come after that.

Well, she could talk about her family. But already she would be getting too personal. Miss Marks would think what anybody would think about her father, who blew the whistle (he was crazy!), and her uncle, who was building a helicopter in the basement (he was crazy!).

She gathered the balled-up paper and carried it out to the recycling bin, just in case Miss Marks loved the environment, which she certainly did, even if she didn't exactly say so.

MISS MARKS BEGAN COLLECTING THE HOMEWORK LETTERS, STARTING WITH MINNIE'S ROW. Minnie sat on her hands to keep them from shaking. She felt like kicking herself for not taking Becky's advice. Now she would find out what happened to the kids at Mojave when they didn't do their homework.

Her stomach began to ache. She kept her eyes on Miss Marks's sandaled feet as they came closer and closer and stopped at Minnie's desk.

Miss Marks's second toes were longer than her first ones. She wore a ring on her left pinky toe. Her polish was pale pink. Her silver sandals had little heels—

"Minnie?"

Minnie raised her head. "I didn't do it," she whispered.

Miss Marks leaned over, turning her ear toward Minnie.

"I didn't do the homework."

Miss Marks smiled. Her teeth were small and perfect,

except for one that turned a little bit out. "You didn't do it *yet*. Right?" she said. "Don't worry, there's no deadline."

She had spoken softly, but the kids nearby had heard and now they were incensed.

"I thought it was due today!"

"No fair!"

"No deadline? You didn't say that!"

Minnie shrank lower into her seat, the blood in her ears and cheeks beating, beating, while Miss Marks collected the rest of the letters. Carl was the only one besides Minnie who hadn't done his. When Miss Marks repeated what she'd said to Minnie, kids all over the room booed and whined.

"Okay, okay," said Miss Marks, holding up her hands. "I see that you're used to deadlines. I'll make sure to give you some."

Had they been tricked? Had they tricked themselves?

"What about points?" said Derek. "Do we get points for doing homework?"

Miss Marks shrugged. "Sure," she said.

"How many?" said Derek.

She cocked her head. "How many do you want? A hundred? A thousand?"

"Huh?"

"I'm a teacher," she said with a big, open smile. "I have all the points in the world."

"Okay, I'll take a million," said Derek.

"You've got 'em," said Miss Marks. "And now I'd better take roll."

Minnie exchanged a troubled look with Amira. Something about all this wasn't working. If everybody got all the points they wanted, how would Miss Marks know what their grades were? And if she forgot to give deadlines, nobody would do the homework.

Minnie began to feel sorry for Miss Marks. She was a nice person, but she didn't know very much about teaching.

She began calling roll, looking each time at the face of the person whose name she had called and staying there for a l-o-n-g time. Minnie thought she would faint waiting for Miss Marks to get to her, but she didn't, and when Miss Marks looked at Minnie and called her name, Minnie felt as if she could stay in the teacher's bright blue eyes forever.

HER PARENTS WERE IN THEIR BEDROOM ARGUING AGAIN. They somehow managed to fight without raising their voices, like dogs with bark collars on. But it was still scary. What if they got a divorce? Then nothing would ever be the same.

So many kids at her old school had divorced parents. Katya's had split up at the beginning of fifth grade. She said it was the worst thing that could ever happen to a kid. She had cried herself to sleep every night because her father already had a girlfriend that he expected Katya to like. Her mother expected Katya to hate her. It was like being the rope in a tug-of-war, she said.

Minnie knocked on Dylan's door.

"What?" he said.

"Can I come in?"

He opened the door enough to stick his head out. His sun-bleached hair hung in his face. He flipped it back. "What do you want?"

"Mom and Dad are fighting," she said. Dylan had

grown so much in one year that looking up at him gave Minnie a crick in her neck.

"So they're fighting," he said. "What's new?"

Minnie waited for Dylan to say something to make it better like he used to, but she wasn't surprised when he didn't. It was all part of the change.

"Do you want to play Monopoly or something?" she said.

"I'm doing my homework," he said. "You'd better do yours."

"I can't," she said. She had tried not to whine, but *I can't* and whining just seemed to go together.

"Little Miss Straight A can't do her homework?" He rolled his eyes. "Too bad." He closed the door, leaving Minnie to stare at the drawing he'd done of a skull and crossbones. KEEP OUT, it said, THIS MEANS YOU!!!!!!!

"You" meant Minnie. Who else? They used to watch *SpongeBob SquarePants* together, eating popcorn out of the same bowl. He taught her how to play chess. He listened when she told him about school. Once he even scared the pee out of a boy who threatened to beat Minnie up.

Now he hated her.

No, he didn't hate her. He acted as if she were invisible, which was worse.

Minnie went back to her room and sat down at her desk, where her purple journal lay waiting.

Miss Marks had begun the journal assignment by talking about questions. Questions were how we learned about our world, she'd said, how we advanced as a civilization. If no one had wondered about the planet, we might still believe that the earth was flat.

Minnie had been hypnotized, not so much about what Miss Marks said but how she said it. As if asking questions was the most exciting, most important and responsible thing a person could do.

While the class called out questions, she wrote them on the board, no matter how silly they were. "Is the sky really blue? How loud is an elephant's fart? Who invented cream cheese? How long would it take to walk around the world?"

When she encouraged the class to ask about things "a little closer to home," they asked why school lunches were so terrible, why the football team sucked, why the eighth-graders were mean, how the seagulls knew when it was lunchtime—and soon the board was covered with Miss Marks's illegible scrawl.

Their homework was to make a list of ten questions about things they really wanted to know. If they really,

really wanted to know why the sky was blue, well, that was all right. But she hoped they would spend some time thinking about their own questions, and not settling for anyone else's.

"Search your mind and heart," she had said as her earnest blue eyes went from face to face. "Someday you will all be working to solve the many problems we adults have passed down to you, but first you need to know how to tackle your own. The way you begin is by asking questions."

Minnie chewed on the end of her pen, trying to think of questions, but her mind and heart just weren't working.

She got up. She went into the kitchen and opened the door to the basement. The lights were off. "Uncle Bill?"

She made her way carefully down the dark steps. A stream of grayish light came through the basement's narrow window. The air was musty and still. Her uncle was sitting on the couch with his head bent over his clasped hands.

Was he praying? Minnie stopped still on the last step.

Her uncle looked up. His eyes held a distant gaze. For a scary moment, it seemed as if he didn't know who she was. Then he smiled his usual lopsided smile. "How goes it?" he said. "How's the new teacher?"

Even to her favorite uncle, Minnie couldn't explain the mess of feelings she had about Miss Marks. Good ones, scary ones, ones she couldn't name. Her feelings changed from moment to moment. Miss Marks excited her, woke up her brain and made her think, but she seemed to expect things that no teacher had ever expected. At least no teacher that Minnie had ever had.

"I don't know yet," she said. "She's . . . different. She wants us to ask all these . . . *questions*. Ten good questions. That's the homework."

Her uncle brushed crumbs off the couch and folded his blanket. The blanket's moth holes made Minnie feel sad, the way she felt passing homeless people on the street. If her uncle didn't shave soon, he was going to look like one of them.

"Ten questions?" He attached his prosthesis and rolled his pant leg down. "Pretty easy homework." He pulled himself to a standing position using his arms and his real leg. He picked up his cigarettes. Minnie followed him into the backyard.

A wide ribbon of stars crossed the sky. They cast a silvery light onto the little fountain that had come in a box from Home Depot. Next to the fountain were two white plastic chairs that looked more empty than they were.

Their old two-story house had been yellow with chocolate-brown trim. It had a big front porch, a huge front lawn, and a pool in the back with two cushy lounge chairs.

This house was beige, beige, beige. It had one floor, a dumb little porch, plastic chairs, and cacti with needles so sharp they could kill you.

Why Mojave?

Did her parents like the desert, or was her father's job at the community college the only one he could find?

"Asking good questions isn't easy," said Minnie.

Her uncle gave her the putting-me-on look. "You're full of questions, Minnie. You're always asking me questions."

"Those are different," she said. "Those are real. Anyway, they don't count. You never answer any of them."

He slid a cigarette out of a crumpled pack. "Sure I do."

"Not the ones about the war."

"Hmmmm," he said, cupping his hand around his cigarette to light it.

"Why do you do that?" said Minnie.

"What?"

"Light your cigarette that way, with your hand around it."

"Wind," he said.

Minnie held out her hand. "There's no wind," she said.

"Not here," he said.

He took a drag of his cigarette and blew the smoke out in a long plume. "That was a question, by the way."

"A *personal* question," she said.

"So you can't ask personal questions?"

Minnie thought about it. "I don't know. I guess we can."

"Well, there you go then," he said.

Minnie looked up at the dark sky and thought there must be at least as many questions as there were stars. So why was the homework so hard to do? Because she wanted to please Miss Marks? Was that it? Or was it because she didn't completely trust her yet? What if Miss Marks shared one of Minnie's questions and the class laughed?

From down the street, a dog began to bark, then Tuffy began to bark and Miss Keller yelled at him.

"Why are you building that helicopter, Uncle Bill?" she said. If he had a good reason, a really good reason, Minnie could tell Dylan that he was wrong, their uncle wasn't crazy.

In the dark it was hard to see the expression on his face. "I'm just trying to figure some stuff out, Minnie," he said. "That's another question, by the way."

"Are you going to fly it?"

"Of course I'm going to fly it," he said.

"You're kidding, right?"

He grinned his lopsided grin. "You think so?"

Minnie looked back at the door to the basement. "How are you going to get it out of there?"

"We lift the top off the house," he said, raising his chin to look at the roof. "And *whoosh*, up she goes!"

He laughed until he started to cough. Then he squished the lit end of the half-finished cigarette between his fingers and put it in his pocket.

"So you're kidding," she said.

"Right," he said. "I'm kidding."

She followed him inside. He sat on the couch and she plunked down beside him. "Help me come up with some good questions," she said.

His eyes got wide. There were red veins running through them, like tiny crooked roads. "Let me get this straight. You want *me* to do your homework?"

"Just this time," she said. "To get me started."

He rubbed his thigh where the fake leg was attached. "Okay," he said. "You got a pencil?"

"Wait!" She raced up the steps, into her room, grabbed her journal and pen, and hurried back downstairs.

She opened her journal. "Ready," she said.

"Okay, here you go. Where did we come from, why are we here, and where are we going?"

Minnie's mind and pen could not keep up. "What?"

"Where did we come from, why are we here, and where are we going?" he repeated, more slowly this time.

Minnie stared at the three questions written in purple ink on the first page of her inquiry journal. "Are those real questions?" she said.

"Minnie girl," said her uncle. "Those are the *only* real questions."

TODAY MISS MARKS'S T-SHIRT WAS ORANGE. LOVE YOUR MOTHER it said over a picture of the earth from space. Her hair stood up in spikes. Her lips were pinkish white, her fingernails the color of Minnie's journal. She sat on the teacher desk, the place she seemed to like best. Her jeans had raggedy hems.

"I can't wait to hear the questions you've come up with," she said. When she crossed her legs in a yoga pose, Minnie's breath caught. She *did* have a tattoo! A tiny rainbow just above her left ankle. "Who wants to start?"

Minnie sat staring at the cover of her inquiry journal, silently begging Miss Marks not to call on her. All she had written on the first page were her uncle's three weird questions.

She listened over the thump of her heart as Miss Marks dropped names into the room like cherry bombs. Jorge? Derek? Maria? No one wanted to read their questions. Minnie wasn't the only one.

"Okay," said Miss Marks. "I understand. You're afraid that someone will laugh at you or think your question is dumb. I know, I know. I've been there."

Minnie sneaked a look at Miss Marks. Had she read Minnie's mind?

"We need to make some rules," she said.

Somebody moaned.

"There's really only one," she said. "Respect." She wasn't laughing now. She wasn't even smiling. "I want you to listen to what your classmates have to say and to think about it, not judge it, *think* about it. I want you to listen not only with your ears, but with your heart."

A couple of the boys snickered.

"Oh, grow up," said Alicia.

Derek's face turned red as a tomato.

"And if you absolutely do not want me to read to the class what you have written," said Miss Marks, "or you don't want me to ask you to read it, just write this on your entry." She went to the board. FYEO, she wrote in big red letters. "For Your Eyes Only."

"I'll start," said Alicia, opening her journal. "Why do sixth-grade boys act like such weenies?"

"You didn't write that!" cried Carl.

"Did too!" said Alicia. She held up her journal page for everyone to see.

"Who's next?" said Miss Marks.

"Why are sixth-grade girls such snot heads?" said Carl.

"Dude!" said Derek.

Miss Marks, back in her yoga pose, waited for the class to settle down. "That doesn't sound like respect to me. We've got some work to do."

She called on a few more kids, who shook their heads.

"Okay," she said. "Here's one of mine." She reached for a journal with a red cover.

"You did the homework?" said Jorge, his brown eyes wide in disbelief.

"Question number one," said Miss Marks, reading from her page. "How will I know if I'm doing a good job?"

Except for an overhead light that buzzed, the room was dead silent. Minnie saw in the faces around her the same astonishment and confusion she felt. Wasn't a teacher supposed to know a thing like that? Didn't all the teachers know when they were doing a good job? They gave tests, didn't they? Then they knew.

Poor Miss Marks. Minnie wanted to console her, to tell Miss Marks she'd feel more confident after she gave them some tests. But what if they didn't do well on their tests? Would Miss Marks get fired?

Maybe that's what she was worried about.

But Miss Marks didn't look worried at all. The look on her face said that she liked her question. She might even be excited about it.

She slid down off her desk and began walking around the room, up and down the rows. The kids had to swivel back and forth in their desks just to see her. "The test of a good question," she said, "is that it doesn't have an easy answer. A good question could have a dozen answers, two dozen! The more the better. Yes, two plus two equals four. But what about 'where did all the dinosaurs go?' And 'what are we all doing here?'"

That last one sounded just like an Uncle Bill question. Minnie couldn't help thinking that Miss Marks and Uncle Bill might make a good couple. *If* her uncle shaved, and *if* he didn't mention that he lived in a basement.

Miss Marks returned to the front of the room. "The point is not to settle for the first answer you come up with. It's to *explore*." She opened her arms wide, as if she were holding a giant balloon. "See where your mind takes you. You don't need to be right. You just need to keep thinking, wondering, asking. Open to surprises."

"I don't get it," whined Jorge. "You're making my brain hurt."

"Good! Good!" cried Miss Marks. "That means you're thinking!"

A few of the kids laughed, but most looked puzzled. Minnie knew exactly how Jorge felt. Her brain was hurting, too.

"Look at your ten questions," said Miss Marks. "And choose one that really *speaks* to you."

That did it. Now half the class was cracking up.

Miss Marks laughed along with them. "Okay, okay, choose the one you think is best."

Minnie looked down at her uncle's three questions. They were all the same. Impossible. She didn't like any of them. Not one of them *spoke* to her. She wished now that she hadn't asked him for help. He spent too much time in the basement. Dylan was right, their uncle was losing his mind.

But he *wasn't*. He talked like a regular person. He listened better than her mother and father, and especially Dylan. What was "crazy" anyway? If you built a helicopter and wanted to fly it out of a basement, did that mean you were crazy?

"Now write that question on its own page," said Miss Marks. "And when I tell you to start, I'd like you to write whatever comes into your mind. No matter how silly it seems, just keep writing until I tell you to stop." Miss Marks looked at her watch, a huge yellow plastic thing that made her arm look like a stick.

Minnie stared at her three questions until they blurred on the page. And then it just came to her, a question that she really didn't have the answer to, but really needed to answer.

On the top of the second page in her journal, in purple ink, she wrote "Is Uncle Bill crazy?"

Minnie was staring at her blank canvas when Mr. Irwin came up behind her. "Just get something on there, Minnie," he said. "A line, some paint. There's nothing more daunting than empty white space."

From her first day at Mojave, Minnie had loved the jumble that was their art room. Every bit of wall and shelf space was taken up with student art—paintings, collages, sketches, and sculpture. It was an exciting, colorful mess and, until this assignment, the place in which Minnie felt most at home. Now it was just a mess.

She waited for Mr. Irwin to go away. When he didn't, she picked up her pencil and drew a circle the approximate size and shape of her face.

"That's it," he said, moving off. "Now keep going."

This morning before school, knowing she would have to sit and stare at her canvas again fifth period, Minnie looked long and hard in the bathroom mirror. She had tried to imagine how she would paint her serious brown eyes. Was there a color called "mud"? She looked closer. Was that a crease between her eyes?

It was! Her mother was right, she did worry too much, and now she was aging prematurely. By next year, she would probably have her first gray hair.

Staring into that mirror as she stared at her canvas now, she had licked her dry, chapped lips. She had counted the freckles that were not disappearing as her mother said they would, twenty-three brown spots that crossed her nose like an army of ticks.

She had combed her fingers through the straight brown hair that hung to her shoulders and covered up the fact that she had the fattest earlobes of anyone she had ever seen. She would never wear earrings, or studs like Miss Marks. When she was old enough not to need permission, she would get an ear lobectomy.

She had run pink gloss over her lips and smiled at herself. Then she had frowned. Then she had made the ugliest face she could make.

That's what she would paint, she'd decided, that ugly face.

But between breakfast and fifth period, she'd lost her nerve. Staring at the circle on her no longer completely blank canvas, she steeled herself to receive her first failing grades, one in art and another in language arts.

That would make her parents sorry they had moved here. Maybe they would even move back to Pasadena, where her father would be a lawyer again, and Minnie would be walking to school with Katya and Becky as if she had never left.

Todd, who had waited almost as long as Minnie, had finally drawn a face. A really ugly face with fangs and mean eyes. She watched him reach for a jar of black paint and dip his brush in. Then her mouth fell open as Todd, whose skin was pale as skimmed milk, painted the face black.

Why would a boy like Todd draw a face like that?

Across the table, Amira sat straight-backed on her stool. She was the only one in the class who could sit all period without slumping. Yesterday, she had finished her sketch of an oval head with a scarf tied under its chin. Minnie was dying to see if Amira had started her face. That was the hard part, the part Minnie could only imagine doing.

She picked up a pencil that called out to be sharpened right this second. The sharpener just happened to be on the wall behind Amira. Staring over her shoulder at Amira's self-portrait, Minnie ground her pencil to a stub.

The scarf Amira had drawn was gorgeous. It was not at all like the plain navy blue one she wore today or any of the others she wore to school. There were birds and flowers and butterflies dancing all over it. As Minnie watched, Amira dipped a brush in yellow paint and filled the circle inside one of her daisies. Amira was a true artist. Her flowers looked like real live flowers. Her butterflies looked like actual butterflies.

Minnie went back to her place. With her sharpened pencil stub she traced and retraced the circle of her face, going round and round until it looked like a broken Slinky.

MINNIE WAS HEADING FOR THE BUS WHEN SHE
FELT A TAP ON HER SHOULDER.

"Minnie?" Amira stood with her heavy leather briefcase weighing her shoulder down.

"Hi!" said Minnie, relieved to see Amira and not Carl
or Derek behind her.

"I was wondering if perhaps you would like to come
to my house one day after school," said Amira.

Minnie almost said "perhaps," but settled for "sure."
The confident, grownup way Amira spoke made a calm
space within the hustle and chatter of their classmates
heading home from school.

"My mother will pick us up and take you home after,"
Amira said. "Would tomorrow be a good day?"

"I'll have to ask," said Minnie.

They exchanged phone numbers and Minnie watched
Amira hurry off toward a long black car waiting at the
curb. Her heart felt light, the way her mother said she

always felt after a good massage. She had a friend, her first friend at Mojave.

Kids rushed past Minnie as if she were a rock in the stream, a small one. Watching Amira climb into the back of the shiny black car, Minnie half listened to conversations that swirled around her.

". . . you didn't! . . . he said what? . . . you're kidding! . . . then my mother . . . the new teacher!"

Minnie tuned in.

"She lives in those condos . . ." said Derek. He was walking between tall Carl and taller Lily, like a tooth that hadn't grown all the way in.

"The pink ones?" said Lily.

"Yeah. On the ground floor. It would be easy."

What would be easy?

Minnie followed them all the way to the bus, then up the steps and inside. The three crammed into a seat in the front. Minnie slid into the one behind them. In the noise and shuffle, she missed what they were saying. But Miss Marks was the only new teacher. They had to have been talking about her.

Then Lily began talking about her brother, who was getting his driver's license, and Carl said he already knew how to drive, and Derek said he was full of the word that Minnie wouldn't say even if she was allowed to, and Minnie sat wondering *what* would be easy.

Were they going to break into Miss Marks's condo? *They were!*

Minnie felt hot and cold all over. Her heart thumped with a sickening beat. Her mind slammed questions around like Ping-Pong balls. What should she do? Tell her father? Mr. Butovsky? Miss Marks?

But what if she was wrong? What if the "it" was something else? Some other "easy" thing? What if she "blew the whistle" and was wrong? She'd be smothered beneath an avalanche of embarrassment too huge to ever dig out of. She would have to quit school.

She would be an eleven-and-a-half-year-old dropout.

Her father was cutting the dead grass with an old-fashioned mower. The bald spot on his head had turned pink in the sun.

"Dad?"

He looked up and smiled, just like he used to. "How's my girl?" he said.

"Okay." She dropped her backpack on the steps. "Can I ask you something?"

He swiped at his sweaty forehead with the back of his wrist. "Of course you may."

She almost changed her mind. It was already clear that her father didn't like to talk about "the whistle-blowing incident," as her mother put it. If he did, he would have explained it to Minnie and Dylan. But Minnie needed to know about it, especially now.

Miss Marks hadn't said that some questions could make you feel like stuffing your mouth with a sock.

Minnie stalled for time. "Let's get a cold drink," she said. "It's hot out here."

They went inside. Her father popped the tops on two cans of Pepsi and handed one to Minnie. "So what's going on?" he said.

She pulled herself up onto the counter, giving her two feet of confidence she didn't have before. "You know when you, um, lost your job?"

"Sure, I know." His forehead twitched, but he didn't look away.

"Well, Miss Marks talks a lot about questions."

"Questions?" He took a long drink. She watched his Adam's apple bob as the Pepsi went down his throat.

"We're supposed to, like, ask the questions our minds

and hearts want answers to and . . ." Minnie rubbed at an invisible spot on her jeans.

"And?"

"Well, I need to know about the whistle-blowing thing." There. It was out.

Her father sighed. "I thought your mother explained all that."

Minnie bit her lip and thought about changing her mind. "She did, sort of." She pushed on. "But Mom never said why. *Why* you did it."

"Ah," he said. He nodded a couple of times, very slowly. He ran his hand over his mouth. He looked at Minnie with the same serious brown eyes she had studied just this morning in the bathroom mirror. Only his weren't the color of mud. His were more like dark chocolate with tiny flecks of almond.

"A young man in our firm was let go," he said. "He was a good lawyer and a hard worker. But two of the partners met behind closed doors and decided to fire him. No reason, except that one of the partner's sons had just graduated law school and needed a job."

"No fair!" said Minnie.

"Exactly," said her father. "That's why I called Truman,

the senior partner. I thought he'd agree with me, but he didn't. I lost my temper. And, well, you know the rest. They fired me as well. I can't say I was surprised. There were other things we didn't see eye to eye on."

"So why did you do it? Why didn't you just . . ." She shrugged.

"Mind my own business? Keep my mouth shut?" He laughed. Then his eyes got serious again. "It wasn't right, Minnie."

Minnie felt a rush of pride for her father. She was glad now that she'd asked him about the whistle-blowing. But she felt sad for him, too, because it had cost him his job.

"You could be a lawyer again," she said. That was a question, too. It just didn't sound like one.

"Maybe I'll just hang out my own sign here in Mojave," he said. "Or write a book."

"About whistle-blowers," said Minnie.

"Good idea. Or your mom could get another job, a second job, and I can make birdhouses. I've always wanted to make birdhouses." He winked.

"Dad?"

"Yes, Minnie."

"Are you and Mom—" She charged ahead. "Do you and Mom still like each other?"

Her father frowned. "Of course we do. What kind of a question is that?"

When he lifted Minnie down off the counter, she felt like a little girl again. She *wanted* to be a little girl, when all she needed to know was how many days before her next birthday, and if she could have a second Dove bar.

MINNIE TOSSED AND TURNED. The full moon came through her window like a spotlight, the kind the police put on criminals when they were trying to get them to talk. Should she tell? Should she not? Back and forth went her mind, until it got tired and stuck on "not."

At 10:17, she went to the window just as her uncle was leaving the house. She watched him bend to pick something off the sidewalk and put it into his pocket. A coin? A cigarette butt? Then, with his hands stuffed into his pockets, he walked off down the street.

Minnie wondered now why she hadn't asked him if she should tell on Carl and Lily and Derek, or what he thought the "easy" thing might be. She could have asked her dad this afternoon, but she'd been thinking about the whistle-blowing thing then. With her arms crossed on the window ledge, she decided to wait for her uncle to return.

When she opened her eyes, her clock said 11:02. She had fallen asleep on her arms. A line of drool ran down onto the window ledge. If her uncle was back, she had missed him.

She got into bed, smoothing her light blanket and fluffing her pillow until it was just right. She lay down and closed her eyes, scratched her knee, turned onto her left side, flipped over onto her right side. Thoughts raced this way, then that, like mice running through the maze of her brain. If she told she'd be a snitch. Even if she was right, no one would ever trust her again.

Not that they trusted her now.

But if she didn't tell somebody and Miss Marks got robbed, Minnie would never be able to look into her teacher's honest blue eyes again.

She awoke with a headache. On top of everything else, she had forgotten to ask her mother for permission to go to Amira's after school.

Her parents' bedroom door was closed. Either they were sleeping—unlikely at 7:15 a.m.—or they were arguing, also unlikely this early, or they were kissing and stuff. But this wasn't likely either, since they weren't getting along.

At the kitchen table, Dylan was slurping up Cheerios. His face was almost in the bowl. Did Dylan need glasses? Then she noticed the graphic novel open on his lap.

"Good morning," she said, just to confirm what a jerk he was. But to her surprise, he said "Morning" back.

She got a bowl and poured herself some Cheerios.

Her mother came into the kitchen and kissed them both on the tops of their heads. "Good morning, my sweeties," she said. Her face was pink, which probably meant nothing. But then her father came in wearing a big smile and a towel wrapped around his waist. He poured himself a cup of coffee and went whistling back down the hall.

So it was option three. Now Minnie was blushing, too, but Dylan went on slurping and reading, oblivious.

It seemed as good a time as any to ask her parents for permission to go to Amira's. In fact, it might be a good time to ask for silver clogs like the ones she had seen on an older girl at school.

She tried for both and got one. "You know we're downsizing, Minnie," her mother said. Minnie was beginning to hate that word. It sounded like they were all shrinking, and she was short enough already. "I'll pick you up. That way I can meet both Amira and her mother."

"They're from some other country," said Minnie.

"Most people are," said her mother with her salesperson smile. "That's the beauty of America. It's a real melting pot."

"I think it's Iraq or maybe Iran," said Minnie. "One of those countries where girls wear scarves all the time."

Her mother's smile tightened at the corners. "Oh," she said. "Well." Frowning, she took a sip of her coffee.

"Well, what?" said Minnie.

"Oh!" said her mother. "Nothing." She patted Minnie's hand. "Better get dressed," she said. "You're going to miss the bus."

The first face Minnie saw on the bus, besides the driver's, was Derek's. He was writing his name through the steam from his breath. Minnie took the empty seat behind him.

What if it was already too late? What if he or they had done the "easy" thing last night? Why hadn't she thought about that until right this minute?

Three stops later, Lily and Carl got on the bus. They plunked down next to Derek. "Hey, dork," said Carl.

"Hey, Curl," said Derek.

"Look, you guys!" said Lily. When she lifted her long dark hair, Minnie saw the three gold studs in her pink and swollen earlobe.

"Copycat," said Carl.

"I was going to get them before Miss Marks came," sniffed Lily. "Ask anybody!"

"Let's see your ankle," said Derek.

"Why?"

"The rainbow tattoo."

"No way," said Lily. "My dad would kill me."

Carl turned to Derek. "So did you go over—?"

The bus stopped with a squeal of brakes and two kids got on. They took the seat behind Minnie, talking so loudly that Minnie couldn't hear Carl and Derek and Lily at all.

When the kids lined up to get off the bus, Minnie slipped in behind Derek. They all clomped down the steps and onto the sidewalk. Lily, flipping back her hair, walked off with Alicia, who'd been waiting for her. Derek went right and Carl went left.

Minnie shuffled off to homeroom. It was hard work being a spy. It curdled the milk in her stomach and made her tired. Her brain felt finished for the day.

"WE'LL START RIGHT OFF WITH SOME FREEWRIT- ING TODAY," SAID MISS MARKS FROM HER PERCH ON THE DESK. Today's T-shirt was black. It said KILL YOUR TELEVISION. A wide black belt with brass studs was threaded through her faded jeans.

Derek's hand shot up.

Miss Marks smiled. "Yes, Derek," she said. "You get points for every entry."

"How many?"

"Ten thousand," said Miss Marks with a glint in her eye.

"Cool!" said Derek.

"Dork," said Carl. "Don't you get it?"

Miss Marks zeroed right in on Carl. "No name-calling, please."

She slid her journal out of the backpack that sat on the teacher's chair. "Let's do ten minutes of freewriting," she said. "No stopping until I say 'time.' Don't worry about organization or spelling, just write whatever comes to mind." She opened her journal and clicked her pen. "Are we ready?"

Derek had already begun, but Minnie could see that he was only drawing pictures.

Minnie couldn't start. All she could think about was what she had decided not to think about anymore, what Derek said on the bus. She wiped the sweat from her pen onto her sleeve. Then she noticed a hangnail that begged to be chewed off.

She glanced up from her journal just as Miss Marks looked up from hers. Miss Marks smiled at Minnie. She held up her pen and pretended to write in the air.

Busted!

Minnie made a line of cursive O's, curling her left arm around the page to hide it. A panic of butterflies flew up from her stomach into her chest. She wrote "I don't know what to write, I don't know what to write" until her hand ached and Miss Marks called time.

"Good work!" said Miss Marks, sliding down off her desk. "I know it's hard to keep that pen moving, but it will get easier. You'll get a good start in class. And I expect you to write at least a page every night for homework. A couple of times a week, I'll collect your journals to take home and read."

Minnie's butterflies clogged her throat and threatened to cut off her wind. *Collect them?* She was actually going to read all their journals? Staring straight ahead, Minnie began tugging the page she had scribbled on out of her journal.

"And remember," said Miss Marks. "Anything you don't want to share gets FYEO at the top."

Minnie kept tearing the page until it was free of the journal. Folding it over, she slipped it into her backpack.

"Now," said Miss Marks, "who would like to share?"

Alicia's hand went up.

"Let's all listen to Alicia's entry," said Miss Marks. "Respectfully." She seemed to be looking at every kid in the class, which wasn't really possible. "Go ahead, Alicia."

Alicia read a poem about horses. It was amazing. Every line rhymed just perfectly. How could she have written such a great poem in only ten minutes? Now Minnie knew there was no hope for her. If this was what Miss Marks expected, she would fail the class for sure.

"Thank you, Alicia," said Miss Marks.

Minnie waited for Miss Marks to say something more, to praise Alicia's perfect poem, but all she said was "Who's next?"

No one volunteered. They all looked like Minnie felt.

If they couldn't write a fabulous poem like Alicia's, why bother?

Then Theresa's hand went up. What a surprise! Theresa was the strangest kid in class. Dressed from head to toe in black, she sat with her long black hair hanging down over her crossed arms. She rarely moved and she never talked, not to anyone.

A swarm of whispers flitted across the room.

"Are we ready?" said Miss Marks, with that same serious look. She waited until all the kids were quiet. "Okay, Theresa."

In a singsongy voice that didn't match her outfit, Theresa began to read a story about a rottweiler named Devil Dog. Somebody snickered and Miss Marks held up her hand for quiet. "Devil Dog lived in a nasty, rotten, broken-down house," Theresa read. "Then some new neighbors moved in next door. They had a cat named Sweetie and three brand-new baby kittens. Two kittens went to good homes, but nobody wanted the third one. Nobody wanted that one except the rottweiler."

Minnie knew what was coming. They all did. She wanted to cover her ears, and would have if Miss Marks hadn't been watching with her everywhere-at-once eyes.

"Devil Dog grabbed the tiny sweet kitten in its

powerful jaws and shook her to death. The end." Theresa closed her journal and laid her crossed hands over the black cover. For what seemed like a long time, the only sound in the room came from the buzzing overhead light.

Miss Marks's blue eyes were very wide. For once, she seemed to have run out of words. "Thank you, Theresa," she said at last. "Who's next?" She waited for what seemed to Minnie a very long time. "No one? Okay, then. Let's thank Alicia and Theresa for being so brave and starting us off." She clapped until a few of the kids began clapping with her, and then some more, and then all the kids were clapping, dispersing the mood that had hung like a black cloud over their heads.

Miss Marks dug into her backpack and took out the letters the class had written to her. Some letters had been put into envelopes. One was pink. One was decorated with hearts. "These were such a pleasure to read," she said. "I feel like I know you now. Thank you so much." Minnie watched her hand each kid's letter back without asking for names. She already knew who they were.

But she didn't know Minnie. Or if she did, she knew her only as the girl who didn't do her homework. Minnie sneaked a look at Amira, who was reading the back of her letter. Whatever Miss Marks had written there had made Amira smile.

Tonight she would write her letter to Miss Marks. And she would do a journal entry, too. If she couldn't think of anything to write, she would do what Becky suggested: she would make something up.

She wouldn't exactly lie. That would be so wrong. Making up something wasn't lying, it was fiction. Fiction was good.

Miss Marks was passing out some fiction books right now. Minnie looked at the cover when Thomas passed hers back. She was disappointed. It was a baby book with a baby title. *Animal Farm* it said over a picture of some pigs and sheep and a rooster wandering around together.

Animal Farm was an important book, Miss Marks said. It was all about power and who gets to make the rules. It was one of the most important books ever written, she said.

Important? A book about animals?

Sitting on her desk with her legs crossed, Miss Marks began to read chapter one while they followed along in their books. Minnie had been right. The book had talking animals in it. One animal, a boar, was in charge of things and he wasn't very happy. He called the other animals "comrades." He told them they were getting a bad deal. They had to work all their lives for the men who only killed them in the end.

"Well," said Miss Marks when she had finished reading the chapter, "what do you think so far?"

"It's sad," said Lily. "I don't like sad books."

"It hurts my brain," said Jorge. "It's like the one Mr. Butovsky read to us. Too many big words."

"It's not really about animals, is it?" said Tuan, who seldom spoke but when he did always said something really smart. He was the smartest kid Minnie had ever had in any class, ever.

Miss Marks smiled. "Isn't it?"

"I don't think so," said Tuan. "There's something else going on."

"There's a lot going on in this book," said Miss Marks. "I'd like you all to read chapter two for homework. It's not a lot of reading. And tomorrow we'll talk about it. George Orwell was—"

The bell rang.

Miss Marks said, "Minnie? Will you stay for a second?"

Minnie wasn't sure she'd heard right. She'd never been asked to stay after class. Staying after was for the bad kids.

She sat with her fingernails digging into her palms as kids filed past her and out the door. She refused to look up, even at Amira, who was taking an extra long time fiddling with the buckle on her briefcase. But finally she too was gone, leaving Minnie in her own little pool of terrified misery.

Minnie stared into her lap, trying to breathe like a normal person. She heard Miss Marks slide off her desk and the soft shuffle of her sandals as she came down the row. When she sat at Thomas's desk, Minnie could smell Miss Marks's perfume, which was sweet and spicy.

She watched Miss Marks's fingers walking toward her across the cover of her journal. She looked up through her tears. Miss Marks was smiling. "I love your name," she said. "Do you know what it means?"

Minnie shook her head. Her tears lost their hold and tumbled down her cheeks.

"Fierce protector," said Miss Marks. "Isn't that great? I looked up the meaning of everybody's name. Yours is absolutely the best." She got up, went to her desk, and came back with a box of tissues, as if crying was no big deal.

Minnie mopped her face and blew her nose.

"I get fierce sometimes," said Miss Marks. "It's kind

of scary, but scary in a good way. Do you ever feel like that? Like screaming?"

Minnie's mind went right to the day she jumped up from this very desk and yelled at the class. "Once," said Minnie, hoping Miss Marks wouldn't ask about it. She tried to keep her eyes on Miss Marks's face, but they kept creeping away as if they had minds of their own.

"Well, I'm going to have to let you go to your next class," said Miss Marks. "I don't want to make you late."

Finally Minnie got it out. "Did I do something wrong?" She had guessed it was the homework she didn't do, but Miss Marks hadn't said a word about it.

"Wrong? Oh, no. I'm sorry. Did I frighten you?" She put a hand on Minnie's shoulder. "I just wanted some time to get to know you a little."

"Oh," said Minnie, another brilliant one-word sentence.

"Off you go then," said Miss Marks. "If you're late, tell Bob—tell *Mr. Irwin* to speak to me."

Minnie fled to her art class just ahead of the bell. She brought her canvas to a table only to stare at it again. She was such a nothing. There it was, right out there on the canvas for everybody to see. She didn't *know* who she was. That was why she couldn't write the letter to Miss

Marks or say more than seven words to her. And that was why she couldn't go beyond that circle on her self-portrait.

The circle she had meant to be the start of a face wasn't a face at all. It was a zero.

AMIRA'S HOUSE WAS AT THE END OF A LONG, SWEEP-
ING DRIVEWAY. Her amma, as she called her mother,
had driven them all the way from school without saying
a word except "Hello. I am pleased to meet you." But she
had shaken Minnie's hand, which made Minnie feel
both grown up and embarrassed. Leaning forward,
Amira's amma drove with both hands clutching the
steering wheel, the tails of her yellow scarf blowing in the
air-conditioned breeze.

Amira didn't talk either. Not until she pulled Minnie
through the huge, sprawling house and into her room,
shutting the door behind them. "Tell me!" she said ur-
gently, grabbing Minnie's hands. "What did Miss Marks
say to you? Why did she keep you after?"

"She wanted to get to know me," said Minnie. "I don't
know. It was weird." Her eyes scanned Amira's bedroom,
which wasn't like any girl's room she had ever seen. On
her wall were huge posters of the night sky. One had all
the stars named, with lines and numbers between them.

Another was of the brilliant universe exploding. Hanging from the ceiling was a planet mobile. Books were neatly set in a tall bookcase. A wide-screen iMac sat on a desk with a polished glass top.

"I was so frightened for you," said Amira. "I could see that you were upset, but I didn't know what you had done."

"I've never been so scared in my life!" said Minnie. "But she was great. She just wanted to know me better."

Amira hugged herself. "I just love Miss Marks."

"I love her, too," said Minnie. At least they had that in common.

Amira took off her scarf, folded it, and laid it carefully in the top drawer of her dresser. "Would you like a soft drink?"

"Okay," said Minnie. She sat down on the edge of Amira's bed to wait, remembering how she and Becky and Katya always sprawled together on each other's beds after school, talking and giggling.

It was strange. Now that she had an almost-friend, she missed her old friends more than ever.

Amira came back with a silver tray. On it were two cans of ginger ale and two fancy glasses filled with ice. She set the tray on her bedside table and sat down beside

Minnie. "I must confess that I often feel nervous in our language arts class," she said.

"Me, too," said Minnie. Amira's way of speaking made Minnie want to sit up straight and choose her words carefully.

"But you have courage," said Amira.

"Me?" said Minnie. Courage? She had about as much courage as the Cowardly Lion.

"Yes! You stood right up and shouted at the students who were misbehaving. I could never do such a thing." Amira touched her chest. "I felt so much admiration for you that day."

Minnie didn't know what to say. If she told her new almost-friend how frightened she had been and how sick she felt afterward, Minnie would surely lose her admiration. Basking in someone's admiration felt good for a change.

"It wasn't easy," said Minnie, cringing inside at the half-truth.

"Surely, it was not," said Amira.

Minnie gazed at Amira's black hair, which was shiny as a crow's wing. If she had hair like Amira's, she could never hide it under a scarf. Did Amira want to hide her hair or did she have to? Minnie knew that the scarves had something to do with religion, she just didn't know what. She and Amira probably had different gods, or different ideas about God.

She shoved all that to the side. She liked Amira. Most of all, she liked that Amira liked her. Even better, Amira admired her.

But if she knew that Minnie did not report something that might hurt their beloved teacher, would Amira admire her then? No, she would not.

They played a game of Scrabble that Minnie thought would never end. Every word was like the turn of a knife in her stomach: "spy," "snitch," "tell," "fear," "teacher." When Minnie had the chance to spell "c-o-w-a-r-d" and use up almost all her letters, she put down only the first three for just eight points instead of the twelve she could have gotten.

The door opened and Amira's amma stuck her head in. "Your mother is here, Minnie," she said.

"Oh!" said Amira. "So soon!" Turning, she knocked against her desk and her mouse hit the floor. Amira's iMac lit up with Facebook.

Facebook!

Amira grabbed the mouse and the screen went dark.

"Amira?" said Minnie.

"Come on," said Amira, grabbing Minnie's arm. "Your mother's waiting."

But Minnie couldn't move. She was shocked. Her own parents wouldn't let her near Facebook.

Amira stopped at the door. She turned to Minnie with troubled eyes. "Please don't tell my mother," she said.

Minnie followed Amira back down the hall that led to the front door, where her mother and Amira's amma were talking. Of course she wouldn't tell. Anyway, it was sort of exciting that Amira had secrets. That they now shared a secret.

". . . so I was wondering," said Minnie's mother, "if *you* had heard anything about Miss Marks. Minnie thinks she's a good—" Minnie watched her mother paste her phony smile on. "Oh, there you are!" she said to Minnie, as if she'd been looking for her all over the house.

They said their goodbyes. Minnie's mother invited Amira to their home, which Minnie had decided not to do the second she saw Amira's room. Why couldn't she mind her own business?

Minnie followed her mother out to their ancient Volvo. She closed her door hoping that for once it wouldn't squeal like a pig, but of course it did. She crossed her arms. Her words came out the way they never did with anybody but her mother. "Why were you and Amira's mother talking about Miss Marks?"

Minnie could tell from the look on her mother's face that she was trying to decide how much to tell her. "We are your parents, Minnie. It's our job to make sure you have good instruction."

"I told you she's a good teacher. A *great* teacher!"

"Yes, I know what you said. But she's only a substitute," said her mother, frowning through the dusty windshield. "She's not a real teacher."

"Yes she is," said Minnie. "She's a real teacher. *You* don't know."

Minnie propped her crummy blue Skechers up on the dash. Once, this had been forbidden, but now the dash was so scratched up that it no longer mattered. Minnie was imagining how a pair of silver clogs would look on her feet. Probably not as good as they looked on that girl at school, but they'd make her a whole two inches taller.

They came to a stop at a red light. "Todd Ingram is in your language arts class, isn't he?" said her mother, asking a question that really wasn't a question since she already knew the answer.

A boy in the backseat of the car beside theirs looked at Minnie, and with his long pink, doggie-looking tongue licked his window. Minnie rolled her eyes and looked back at her mother.

"Yes, Todd's in my class. Why?"

"Probably nothing."

Which of course meant Something. *"What?"*

Her mother glanced over with that same cautious look on her face. "Well, his mother has a few concerns about Miss Marks."

"What concerns?" Ever since Minnie's father had said he had some "concerns" about Uncle Bill, Minnie hated that word. It wasn't plainspoken.

The light changed. The car beside them drove off, the boy making crazy faces through the back window. "Is it true she wears blue jeans every day?" her mother said.

"They aren't called blue jeans, Mom," said Minnie. "They're called jeans."

"Is that what she wears?"

"She wears cool jeans. Like the ones you brought from California and never wear."

"The ones with the studs? You're kidding!"

"Not just those!" said Minnie, trying to get out of the hole she seemed to be digging for Miss Marks. "She has other ones, too."

"Mrs. Ingram says she has a tattoo."

"Mrs. Ingram has a tattoo?" Minnie giggled hysterically. She knew that her mother meant Miss Marks, but the thought of Mrs. Ingram with a tattoo was just too funny.

Her mother waited, unsmiling.

"It's just a tiny rainbow," Minnie said, her laughter dissolving like bubbles in the dishwater.

They pulled into their driveway. Her mother turned off the engine and gathered up her purse.

"Why does it matter what Miss Marks wears?" said Minnie.

Her mother frowned and opened her door. "It just does," she said. "She looks like a—" The door slammed shut.

"She looks like a *what*?" cried Minnie, but her mother with her slim blue suit and her "professional" hair was already walking away.

"WHAT ARE THESE FOR?" SAID MINNIE, POINTING AT TWO ROUND BLACK PLASTIC PIPES HER UNCLE HAD ATTACHED TO THE HELICOPTER'S INSECT LEGS.

His answer came up from underneath, where he was lying on his back. "That's where you put the ammunition," he said.

Minnie wasn't sure she'd heard right. "Ammunition? Like bullets?"

His answer was slow in coming. "Well, yeah, like bullets."

Minnie got down on her hands and knees so that she could see him. "Does it have to have guns?"

"Of course it does," he said, grunting as he got himself up off the floor. "It's an attack helicopter."

"But not real guns," she said, scrambling to her feet. "Right?"

He grinned and mussed her hair. "Not real guns," he said.

Her heart settled. If her uncle were really crazy, there

would be real guns and this would be a real helicopter. But it wasn't. It couldn't be. It was made out of canvas and plywood. It didn't even have a steering wheel, or whatever it was that steered the thing.

But the longer her uncle worked on the "chopper," the more worried Minnie got, and the more worried she got, the more she wanted to know about her uncle and the war. She decided to try what Dylan called an end run, a sneaky kind of football play to move the ball closer to the goal. "You know that journal assignment I told you about?"

He glanced at Minnie and back at the chopper. "Yeah?"

"Well, I'm *really* trying to do a good job on it," she said. "I *really* want to get an A."

Her uncle took a step away from the helicopter and frowned at it. Something wasn't right. "Yeah?"

"We're supposed to write about our family," said Minnie.

Now she had his attention. "You are? Why?"

Minnie shrugged. "I dunno." She couldn't meet her uncle's eyes.

He looked older and even more tired when he frowned. "Some people might call that an invasion of privacy," he said.

"Oh, no, you don't have to worry about that," said Minnie, rushing through the lie so she wouldn't feel it so much. "She promised that our entries would be private."

Her uncle leaned over. He captured her eyes with his that were now a sharp, bright green. "Minnie? What exactly did you mean when you said that *I* didn't have to worry?"

Her insides were twisting into pretzels. The voice that she meant to sound normal came out small and wavery. "The only one I didn't write about yet is you," she said.

"Aha," he said. He stood looking at her with his hands on the hips of his faded fatigues. One pant leg hung empty. The fact that he didn't have his leg on made everything worse. She felt like running. Then she felt bad about that because her uncle could no longer run.

She had made a terrible mess and didn't know how to get out of it.

"Come over here, Minnie," her uncle said. He sat heavily on the couch and patted the cushion beside him. She sat with her head down and her hands clamped between her knees. "I don't want you writing about me, you know that."

She nodded, miserable.

"But it's time that I answered some of your questions," he said. "About . . . about what happened over there. It isn't fair to keep you in the dark."

"I lied about the assignment," said Minnie in an almost-whisper.

"Yeah, I figured," he said.

They sat for a while looking at the helicopter that loomed over them like a bad dream. Around their feet were the remains of her uncle's breakfast, a crust of white bread with peanut butter on it. The GOOD DAY, SUNSHINE coffee cup that her mother brought down each morning filled to the brim with coffee and milk was empty. Whenever Minnie offered to take her uncle his coffee, her mother said she would spill it. Minnie guessed that her mother just wanted to spend some time with him. She never came right back up.

Minnie wondered what her mother and uncle talked about. Did they talk about "getting Bill's life together"? That was what she'd overheard her father say, as if her uncle's life was a jigsaw puzzle with all the pieces scattered.

"I was a pilot in Iraq, Minnie," her uncle said. "You know that part, and you know I was in a crash. That's how I lost my leg."

She nodded.

"What you probably don't know is that I flew what's called a gunship."

"Like that one, right?" said Minnie, looking up at the huge black helicopter.

Her uncle's laugh sounded as if he'd stuck a pin in himself. "Yeah," he said. "Sort of like that one."

"Was it scary?"

"Big-time," he said. "But worse for the people on the ground."

Minnie almost couldn't say out loud what came to her then. She looked at his red-rimmed eyes and flinched. It was as if he already knew what her question would be. "Did you kill people?"

He nodded, the expression in his eyes as dark and sad as she had ever seen. The thought that he might cry terrified her. "That's what goes on in war, Minnie," he said. "People kill people."

"But not . . . *people*, right?"

"Civilians?" He looked down at his hands. "Sometimes."

Minnie sat with that, hunched over as if her heart needed protecting.

"But you just flew the helicopter, right? You didn't shoot the guns."

Her uncle looked up from his hands and straight into her eyes. "It's the same thing, Minnie."

Hugging her knees, Minnie laid her forehead down. Her lip quivered. She wanted to cry, needed to cry, but what she felt for the people and for her uncle, and even for herself, was beyond the relief of tears. She didn't want to know this. She didn't want to know that her uncle had killed people, and she couldn't take her question back. It was too late.

THE UGLY DRAWING LANDED SOMEHOW IN HER HANDS. Minnie didn't see who gave it to her, but it had obviously gone to other kids first. The lined paper was wrinkled and smeared with dirty fingerprints.

RAGHEAD said the block letters written across the top. Underneath was a crude sketch of a girl wearing a scarf and dragging a briefcase behind her.

Minnie's heart raced. She looked wildly around for the trash can that always sat next to the water fountain but wasn't there today. She crumpled up the awful thing and stuffed it into her pocket. After school she would tear the picture up. Burn it!

Who would draw such a mean thing? Was it somebody in their language arts class or in another class Amira had?

Derek! He was drawing this just the other day in his journal. She had *seen* him.

Not exactly. She had watched him start to draw. She had not seen *what* he had drawn. She could almost feel her father's hand on her shoulder, slowing her down. He would tell her not to jump to conclusions. You had to have evidence to convict a person of wrongdoing.

When she got to Room 2, Amira was already inside. Had she seen the drawing? Minnie didn't think so. On Amira's face was her same patient, solemn look. Minnie breathed a sigh of relief and went to her desk.

"Settle down, settle down!" said Miss Marks. "What's going on? You're like popcorn today. Carl? Derek?" She put her finger to her lips. "Okay, that's better."

As Miss Marks scanned the room with her usual smile, relief washed through Minnie. She hadn't seen the drawing either. Minnie didn't think she would be smiling if she had.

Miss Marks continued in a quiet voice, which made the students listen harder. "I'm going to give you a whole twelve minutes to write today," she said, as if she were passing out candy, "but you may stop at ten if you need to. Today I'll be taking your journals home."

Minnie opened her journal to the page that said "Is Uncle Bill crazy?" Back and forth went her pen through that question until it disappeared. She turned the page. There was evidence of the page she'd torn out in the few shreds still left. She tore these out. The next page had three sentences following the question "Are all dogs good?"

"Tuffy is the name of our neighbor's dog. The neighbor's name is Beth Keller. She is moving away."

It was the dumbest, most juvenile thing she had ever written in her life. She quickly flipped to the next page, which was blank.

She watched her pen write "My uncle Bill was in the Iraq war."

For the rest of the twelve minutes, she sat staring at that one sentence, thinking about what it meant, how much more there was behind those eight words. But she could not write anything else. Instead, she kept sneaking looks at Derek's journal to see if he was drawing pictures, but he wasn't.

"Time!" called Miss Marks. "Who would like to share?"

A girl whose name Minnie could not remember read her entry. Her question had been "What do I know about apples?" Miss Marks had the tiniest frown between her eyes as the girl read a list of apple names and why she liked Fujis the best.

Two more kids shared. One wrote about having to clean her room, the other one wrote about her goldfish. Their entries were better than the one about apples, but not by much.

Then Miss Marks asked Jorge if he would read his. She had been happy to see that his entry didn't have FYEO on top, she said, because she was sure the class would like to hear it.

In a quiet, shaky voice, Jorge read what he wrote about the dress code and why he thought it was wrong that they couldn't wear T-shirts with writing on them and pants without belts.

Just then, the door opened and Mrs. Brennan, the librarian, came in. "Excuse me, class," she said. She went to Miss Marks and, with her back to the class, said something they couldn't hear. Miss Marks's face became pinker and pinker until it matched the big pink tongue on her T-shirt.

Mrs. Brennan turned to the class. She was a nice lady who never raised her voice, even when the kids talked too loud. Sometimes she brought homemade cookies, which you had to eat outside. Today she looked as if she had eaten them all herself and had a stomachache. "Would you please take out your *Animal Farm* book and pass it to the front?"

The sound of zippers almost hid the whispers that shot through the room. Why was Mrs. Brennan taking their books away?

But it was not until she had left with the thirty books and Todd Ingram to help carry them that Alicia asked, "Why did she do that?"

Miss Marks had blotches of pink still left on her cheeks. "I blew it," she said. "*Animal Farm* isn't on the sixth-grade reading list."

"But I read the whole thing last night!" blurted Tuan, who had never spoken before without raising his hand. "It was easy."

"I don't think difficulty is the problem," said Miss Marks.

"Then what is?" said Lily.

Miss Marks pinched her lips together until they turned white. She looked at the floor and shook her head. Then she lifted her head and said, "It's not considered appropriate."

"Then what's it doing in the library?" said Alicia.

Miss Marks shrugged. "I'm guessing that it's meant for eighth grade."

"But I'm halfway through the book!" said one of the two Marias, who never spoke out of turn either. "I want to know what happens next!"

Miss Marks lifted an eyebrow. She gazed around the

room, stopping at a face here, a face there. Then she seemed to make up her mind. "Shall I just tell you the story?"

Their response was unanimous. They settled down and listened to Miss Marks tell the story that was all about greed and injustice, and not a baby story at all. Minnie wondered if her father had ever read it. It was his kind of book.

"Why is it only for the eighth grade?" asked Tuan when Miss Marks had finished.

"I don't know," said Miss Marks. "I guess you're not supposed to be able to understand it yet." On the right-hand side of the board she wrote "greed." Under it she wrote "injustice."

Then they were all talking. Well, almost all. Not Minnie or Amira, and not Theresa. "Let me tell you about greed!" said Lily. "My big sister gets all the new clothes. The rest of us get her hand-me-downs!"

"Come to my house for dinner if you want to see greedy!" said Carl. "We kill over the last drumstick."

Then Jorge went on and on about how "injust" his father was. "Why are grownups always right even when they're not?" he said.

Miss Marks smiled. "Unjust," she said. "That's a very good question, Jorge. Don't forget to write it in your journal."

Then they were talking all at once about greedy people and people who didn't play fair, something they never did in any other class. Miss Marks tried to calm them down, to get them to share one at a time. But it was hard, and before long, Mr. Trimmer next door was banging on the wall.

"Pass your journals to the front, please," said Miss Marks, and the bell rang.

Safely inside a locked stall in the girls' room, Minnie retrieved the balled-up drawing from her pocket and threw it in the toilet. As the water began to uncrumple it, the hateful word and picture smeared. She quickly flushed the toilet and watched as the ugly thing swirled and went down.

There. Done.

No!

Minnie leaned over and stared into the bowl, but of course the drawing was gone. The *evidence* was gone. What had she been thinking? Now Derek, or whoever drew it, could never be convicted. Minnie had destroyed the evidence.

She opened the door. Amira was washing her hands at the sink. Their eyes met in the mirror. "Are you all right, Minnie?"

Minnie didn't know what to say. She was not all

right, but admitting it meant having to explain to Amira why she was not all right. Or telling a lie, which, no matter what Becky said, was a bad idea.

"You didn't see the drawing the kids were passing around?"

Amira shook her head.

Minnie let out the breath she didn't realize she'd been holding.

Two girls who looked like twins came in. They were each about six feet tall with three feet of blond hair hanging down their backs.

"Come," said Minnie, pulling Amira by the hand out into the hall choked with kids.

"What about the drawing?" said Amira.

"Nothing," said Minnie too quickly. "It was just some silly thing. I flushed it down the toilet."

Amira frowned.

"We'd better hurry. We're gonna be late," Minnie said. It wasn't true, and it didn't erase Amira's frown. She was just too smart.

But once they got to the art room, found their canvases, and took them to one of the long tables, Amira's frown disappeared. She had gotten caught up in her painting.

Minnie stared off into space. She shouldn't have thrown away the drawing. She should have turned it in to the office. What she'd thought of as smart and even a little bit brave was just cowardice.

Who was the bigger coward? The kid who did the drawing and didn't sign his name or the one who didn't track that kid down?

Minnie picked up a paintbrush, determined to put something on her white canvas. She was terrified that Mr. Irwin would send it home with her to finish over the weekend. On the bus would be other kids whose portraits were finished. No way could she hide the stupid zero of her face.

She dipped her brush in yellow, which was a chicken color for what she had in mind. She rinsed the brush. Hesitating over the red, she went at last to the pot of bright green. Over the circle of her face, she painted a huge green question mark.

The butterflies were back, beating their wings high in her throat as if she had actually done something. It *felt* like something, she just didn't know what.

She rinsed out the green paint, and before she lost her nerve went for the blue. Dripping just a little, a blue question mark appeared next to her right ear. Then another green one next to the blue, an orange one next to that, and finally, over her left ear, a vermilion red question mark.

She had worked without thinking. All she knew was that this twelfth year of her life was a whirlwind of questions: Why had her father lost his job? Was Uncle Bill crazy or just sad? Had her mother really changed, or was it just her hair? Did her brother really hate her now? Would she lose her two best friends forever? Did God really see everything she did? Who drew the ugly picture? Was Miss Marks a good teacher? What was a good teacher anyway?

"Wow, Minnie, that's quite a change," said Mr. Irwin, standing behind her. "Nice, bright primary colors. You're really getting somewhere."

Amira was smiling as if Mr. Irwin had complimented her. "I like it," she said. "It looks the way I feel a lot of the time."

"You do?" said Minnie, surprised that Amira, who seemed so confident and . . . *together*, didn't have all the answers.

"You know that drawing you told me about? I thought you were going to say that it was of me." Her dark eyes filled with tears and she blinked them back.

"No!" said Minnie. "It wasn't you. Don't worry. It wasn't you. Really."

Amira's smile reminded Minnie of her Grandmother Steele, whose smile always had sadness mixed up in it. She watched Amira losing herself in her self-portrait. Her face relaxed. She looked sort of dreamy. Minnie looked back at her own portrait. She was beginning to like it, too.

She liked that the girl—the girl who was really herself—wasn't insane. She just had a lot of questions. The girl wasn't miserable about it because she had a feeling that she'd find the answers, if not right now then sometime. But it was hard to convey all that with a fat brush.

She reached for a pencil and drew a thought bubble over her head between the green and blue question marks. "Just thinking," she printed inside it.

She sat back and studied her painting. She loved it. She was over the top with love for it.

But of course she couldn't say that. So when a boy, a cute boy, walked by and said "Cool" and her heart did this little backflip, all Minnie could manage, after clearing her throat, was "M-m-m-m."

Miss Marks was not smiling. She sat on her desk as usual. She nodded at each of them as they came in, but all the sparkle was gone from her eyes. The stragglers who had come into the room laughing took their seats quietly. They all sat waiting for Miss Marks to speak, to start the class, but she didn't say anything. Neither did her blank black T-shirt.

Minnie had gone to only one funeral in her life, her Grandfather Steele's. She had been five years old. She had kept waiting for her grandfather to get out of the box he was sleeping in. She was tired of sitting still and being shushed. She wanted to wake her grandfather up.

This was more or less how Minnie felt now. She wanted to raise her hand and ask Miss Marks what was wrong. Something clearly was, but of course she couldn't ask.

Miss Marks cleared her throat. "You may not have noticed that I've added a new word to our list on the board," she said. "The word 'prejudice.'" She turned toward the white board and there it was, below "greed" and "injustice," the words from *Animal Farm* that had gone up the day before. "I'm going to ask you to write about that word in your journals today." She got up and went to the board. "What is prejudice?" she wrote. "If you are sitting in the first row, will you please come up and get your journal?"

Minnie and the other kids in her row stood up like silent soldiers, found their journals, and marched back to their seats. Without having to be asked, Amira's row stood and did the same, and then the other three rows. Minnie liked an orderly classroom, but this was too weird.

What was going on? Why had Miss Marks changed? And why did they have to write about her question instead of one of their own?

She opened her pitiful journal. On the page that began with "My uncle Bill was in the Iraq war," she found a penciled note from Miss Marks: "I'm glad he's back. My brother will be home in January, but only for a leave. You know how I feel about war. What are your thoughts?"

"I hate war," wrote Minnie and underlined her sentence twice.

"Ten minutes of thoughtful writing," said Miss Marks,

looking at her big yellow watch. "Twelve minutes if you can do it. Start now."

Minnie turned to a new page. She wrote Miss Marks's question on the first line, taking her time. She kept her pen on the page. She didn't dare look up. She thought about the disgusting drawing of Amira wearing her scarf. "I hate prejudice," she wrote.

Okay, so that was a start. But then she was stuck. Wasn't it prejudiced to hate prejudice? So she wrote that question and thought about it. It was okay to hate bad things, right? And prejudice was a bad thing. And then she was off, trying to write as fast as the thoughts tumbled into her brain. When Miss Marks said "Time," Minnie was shocked. She had written for ten, no *twelve*, whole minutes.

"Who would like to start?" said Miss Marks.

No one volunteered.

Minnie kept her eyes locked on the cover of her journal. *Don't call on me, don't call on me, please don't call on me.*

"Alicia?"

Alicia shook her head.

"Theresa?"

Theresa didn't even look up.

Miss Marks sighed. She slid down off her desk. "Okay. I'm sorry. I'm not in a very good mood today. I'm very"—she looked up at the light fixture that was missing a tube as if the word she needed was there—"sad," she said. "On Saturday afternoon as I was finishing up your journals, I found something that really upset me. At first I thought it was a note that had been folded up and stuck between the journals. But when I opened it, I saw that it was a drawing."

Minnie's heart began to race. She *couldn't* have found the ugly drawing. Minnie had seen it go down the toilet.

"The drawing was very crude," she said. "But it was clear that it meant to depict me. Me and another woman."

The room was deathly quiet.

"There were words on the drawing, including my name, all misspelled." She smiled then, a little, and shook her head. "What a way to break a language arts teacher's heart."

She began walking back and forth with her arms crossed. "Being the object of someone's prejudice is not fun," she said. "In fact, it stinks." She stopped and went to the board. "Let's take a look at the word," she said. "Let's break it down."

"Pre," she wrote. "Can somebody help me with this?"

"Before," said Alicia. "It's a prefix." Satisfied, she flipped her hair back.

"Thank you, Alicia," said Miss Marks.

"Judge," she wrote.

Lily waved her hand. "I know! I know! Deciding what's good or bad," she said. "Like on *American Idol*. You know, the judges."

"Thank you, Lily," said Miss Marks. "So what happens then when we put these two together, 'pre' and 'judge'? If a person is prejudging, what is she doing?"

She? Was the person who wrote the note a *girl*? Minnie couldn't believe it. But Miss Marks had used "she" instead of "he" before in that same way. Was that correct "usage," as her fifth-grade teacher used to say? Did it mean Miss Marks wasn't a very good language arts teacher after all?

Miss Marks repeated her question: "If a person is prejudging, what is he doing?"

Now Minnie didn't know what to think. He, she. Next she'd be saying "it"!

Tuan raised his hand.

"Yes, Tuan?"

"If a person is prejudging, he is making a judgment *before*," he said.

Miss Marks's eyes lit up for the first time all period. "Before what?"

"Before he knows anything about . . . about whatever it is," said Tuan.

"Exactly," said Miss Marks. "The person who drew the picture has apparently decided, without knowing one way or the other, that I am gay."

Eyes widened, all breathing seemed to have stopped.

She went to her desk and sat in her usual yoga pose. "My sexual orientation is, of course, nobody's business. Nor is yours."

The word "sexual" hung in the air like a plum ripe for picking, but nobody made a sound.

"Now, I am an adult. I can get over this. I can think about it as somebody's idea of a prank, a bad joke. But I worry that something like this could happen to a student in this school, to somebody who seems 'different' for some reason. That child might be seriously damaged, psychologically damaged. And that," she said, frowning, "is unacceptable and very, very wrong."

A boy in the far corner raised his hand.

"Yes, Diego?"

"Who did it? Who made that drawing?"

"I don't know," said Miss Marks, and for the first

time all period, she smiled. "Whoever it was didn't sign it. Well, it wasn't very good art. I wouldn't have signed it either." She went to her backpack and pulled out a paperback book. "Not that I'd have done such a thing in the first place."

She held up the book. It had a green cover. "There's another book that I think you should read. It's called *To Kill a Mockingbird* by Harper Lee. There's only one copy in our school library because it's not used as a textbook, but our town library has three copies and some of you just might have a copy at home. This one is mine. When I read it many years ago, it answered all my questions about the nature of prejudice, and it just might answer yours as well."

The bell rang. "Please pass your journals to the front," said Miss Marks. "Tomorrow we'll talk about how to turn one of your questions into an essay."

"You were writing furiously today," Miss Marks said as Minnie passed her desk. "Right up till the end. I'm proud of you."

Minnie ducked her head. "Thanks," she said.

It wasn't until the beginning of her art class when Minnie was once again staring at her self-portrait that she remembered, with a stab of real pain, that she had not written FYEO on the top of her entry.

AMIRA SLID OFF HER STOOL AND WENT TO THE
BACK OF THE ROOM. Minnie looked over at Amira's
self-portrait, still just a scarf without a face.

"You did a great job on the scarf," she said when
Amira came back carrying a sheet of paper she'd torn off
the big roll.

Amira smiled. "Thanks." She laid her painting on the
white paper and began to wrap it.

Minnie was surprised. "Aren't you going to finish?"

"It is finished," said Amira.

"But it doesn't have a face," said Minnie.

"No," said Amira, taping the paper together. "It
doesn't."

Minnie shut up. It was like Amira had put a double
period at the end of her answer. The painting was finished
and that was that. Amira was in a bad mood, or maybe
wasn't feeling well. There were dark circles under her eyes,
as if she hadn't slept.

Minnie leaned toward her. "Are you okay?"

Amira's frown had a sad lining. "Yes," she said, taping the ends of the paper together.

Minnie picked up her pencil. She had planned on sketching in the eyes on her portrait today. She had even looked extra long at her eyes in the mirror this morning, studying their shape and size and color, which she decided could be burnt umber.

Was Amira really finished or was she, like Minnie, afraid of drawing her own face?

But Amira would have had to show it to Mr. Irwin. She would have had to get permission to take it home. So it was "finished." Minnie couldn't help thinking that Amira had pulled what her father would call "a fast one." Now she was free to go on to the next assignment, while Minnie was stuck finishing this one.

So lightly that she could barely see the line, she sketched an eye. Too small. Too far to the right. She erased the eye and tried again. This one looked like it belonged on a fish. She erased it.

What were the rules for doing a self-portrait anyway? Mr. Irwin had never told them. Did a self-portrait have to look exactly like the person who painted it? Some of the portraits Mr. Irwin had shown them sure didn't. Not unless the artist really did have a greenish-yellow face and one big black eyebrow.

Minnie drew another thought bubble and wrote "Who decides?" inside it. With just five minutes left of class, she had four more thought bubbles and still no face. She picked up her portrait and took it to the front of the room where Mr. Irwin was tidying up. She waited until he looked at her.

"I need help," she said.

He looked at her painting. His face never gave away what he thought. "How can I help?"

"I'm stuck," she said.

"Stuck how?"

"I can't do a face."

"I see."

"Can it be finished if it doesn't have a face?"

She could tell that he could tell she was thinking about Amira's self-portrait.

"I don't know," he said. "Can it?"

Minnie felt like kicking the table. She hated that kind of answer, an answer that wasn't an answer.

"It's finished when you decide that it's finished," he said. "You're the artist."

Was that true? It sounded right, but it left it all up to her, which wasn't what she wanted at all.

"We could ask the class," he said. "But you wouldn't want that, would you?"

"No!"

"And even if the vote was yes, you still wouldn't be sure. Would you?"

She shook her head.

"So live with it for a while," he said. "Let the painting tell you what to do."

She took it back to the table. She drew another thought bubble over the faceless girl's head. "Will I ever be finished?" it said.

In the pool of her desk light, Minnie's hand hovered above her letter to Miss Marks like a . . . well, like a helicopter. She couldn't start without sounding dumb. She couldn't think of things to say. She wanted to write something about herself that Miss Marks would find beautiful and meaningful. She wanted Miss Marks to admire her, like Amira admired her, even if it was for the wrong reason.

She had finished all her other homework after school, but had again left the letter assignment for "later." It was almost eight o'clock. Her father had gone to teach his night class, her mother was at a meeting, and Dylan was hogging the TV. Outside, the wind was blowing up dust. A storm was on its way.

That was another bad thing about the desert: flash floods.

She could always write about the weather. What kind of weather she liked or hated. But that was so dumb.

She could write about Facebook, if she knew

anything about Facebook. What was really on her mind, what had been on her mind all day, was how sad Miss Marks had been. If she were Miss Marks, she'd walk right out of Mojave Middle School and never come back. But the thought that Miss Marks might actually do that saddened Minnie to the point of despair. It reminded her of the time they had to take their old cat, Peaches, to the vet and she never came home again. So Minnie started writing about Peaches until she realized she wasn't writing about herself at all.

She tore up what she had written and went downstairs.

Her uncle looked up from the book he was frowning over. It was one of his big fat aircraft books that had no pictures, just lots of words and numbers and graphs.

"Guess who was just down here?" he said. "Dylan!" When her uncle smiled, his whole face changed. "I swear the kid's grown a foot in a couple of weeks."

Minnie frowned.

"What's with the face?" said her uncle.

"I'm shrinking," she said.

"You're not shrinking," he said. "Kids don't shrink. Only old people shrink."

Minnie sat down on the arm of the couch. She was happy for her uncle, but jealous. Not because Dylan had grown so much—well, that, too—but because Dylan and Uncle Bill were both *boys*. They could talk about boy things, like what to do with all the spare parts their uncle collected. "What did Dylan want?"

"Help with his skateboard."

Minnie launched into the reason she had come down here in the first place. Dylan wasn't the only one who needed some help. "You'll never believe what happened in language arts today!"

"I might," said her uncle.

She told him about the raghead drawing. She told him about having it show up in her hands like a grenade, and how she had flushed it down the toilet. She told it all breathlessly, as if it were happening right now, which was how it felt.

"Like they say, 'good riddance to bad rubbish,' huh?"

"But there was another drawing!" said Minnie. "It was folded and stuck between our journals. Miss Marks found it and it was of her!"

Her uncle's frown cut a ditch in his forehead. "Not good," he said. He tossed his empty cigarette pack into the paper bag he used for trash.

"I think I know who did it," said Minnie. "A boy named Derek."

Her uncle opened a new pack of cigarettes. "What makes you think it's him?" he said, getting up from the couch.

Minnie followed him outside. The wind blew her hair across her face. She pushed it back and told her uncle what she'd heard Derek say days ago on the bus. "I thought he was going to break into Miss Marks's condo, but do you know what I think now?"

Her uncle cupped his hand around his cigarette and lit it. "Wind," he said, and winked at her. He took a big puff. The wind snatched the smoke as it left his mouth. "So what do you think now?" he said.

"I think Derek went over there and peeked in the window!"

"Hmmmm," said her uncle with his forehead bunched up.

"And that's where he saw Miss Marks with a . . . with a woman!"

"Hold on a minute," said her uncle. "How do you know this Derek guy isn't just making the whole thing up?"

Minnie plunked down in one of the plastic chairs, which was wet from the sprinkler, and leaped back up.

"Well, I don't know for sure. If I knew for sure, I'd turn him in."

Would she? And risk what little chance she had of ever being liked? Little Miss Goody-Goody would. That's exactly what *she* would do.

Her uncle laid a hand on her shoulder. "I think Miss Marks can take care of herself, Minnie. She did what any good teacher would do." He laughed as if he might be remembering his own school years. "She made a lesson out of it."

The door opened and her mother came outside hugging herself. "What are you two doing out here? It's cold!"

Minnie had been so caught up in telling her story that she hadn't even felt the cold. Now she did. She went inside to get her hoodie. Her mother's purse and keys were on the kitchen counter along with a piece of paper with some names and phone numbers on it.

Minnie put on her hoodie and hurried back outside.

"Can they do that to a teacher?" she heard her uncle say.

"Do what?" said Minnie.

Minnie's mother frowned at her like Miss Keller frowned at Tuffy when he got in her way. "Nothing."

"You're talking about Miss Marks, aren't you?" said Minnie.

"I don't want you worrying about it, Minnie," she said, hooking Minnie's hair behind her right ear. Minnie shook it out. "Let me do the worrying about this one, okay?"

"But she's my teacher!" said Minnie.

Tuffy began to bark, scratching his nails against the wooden fence that ran between the two houses.

"Keep your voice down, Minnie," said her mother.

"She has a point, Lin," said her uncle. "Whatever happens to Miss Marks happens to her. And the rest of the kids."

"Bill, I wish you wouldn't—"

"Tell me," Minnie insisted. "I want to know."

Her mother sat down like she weighed a ton. She didn't even seem to realize that the chair was wet. "I just met with several of the parents. They want Miss Marks replaced," she said. "She's just too controversial."

"Ah, yes," said Uncle Bill. "Small-town politics."

"Replaced? Miss Marks?" cried Minnie. "Mom! You can't let that happen."

"Calm down, Minnie," said her mother. "I didn't say she was being let go. I said there are some unhappy parents who are getting together and talking, that's all. It's not up to me, Minnie, or any of us parents. It's up to the administration. I suppose Miss Marks will be given a warning, and if her teaching doesn't improve? Well, I just don't know."

"Well, I do," said Minnie. "I know she's a good teacher. A wonderful teacher!"

Her mother made a prune face. "There are things you don't know, Minnie."

"There are things *you* don't know!" shouted Minnie.

"You are not to talk to me in that voice!" said her mother.

"Fight nice, girls," said Uncle Bill.

Minnie stomped behind her mother and uncle into the basement.

"Are you coming up?" her mother said.

"No," said Minnie with her back turned. "I want Uncle Bill to show me something on the computer."

Without having to see, Minnie knew that her mother's hands were on her hips. "What do you want to look at, Minnie?"

"Nothing," said Minnie. "It's just this site where you can send birthday cards and stuff."

"Oh," said her mother. "Well, I guess that's all right."

When her mother had gone upstairs, her uncle gave her a look. "Birthday cards?"

"Facebook," she said.

He reached for his laptop and opened it. "You need an account to get in," he said. He typed in the URL. "Okay, here it is. I don't want an account. Do you?"

"I don't think so," said Minnie. "Can't we make up a name?"

Her uncle typed "Daisy Pickle" in the name space, then filled out the rest of the questions with made-up facts. "Okay, we're in," he said. "So here it is. It's just a bunch of people trying to be friends with each other. Who does Daisy Pickle want to 'friend'?" he said.

"Amira Ahkbari," said Minnie.

"Iraqi?" her uncle said, frowning.

"I don't know," said Minnie. "I forgot to ask her. What difference does it make?"

"Ahkbari with an h?" he said.

"I think so."

Her uncle typed in Amira's name and she appeared on the screen like magic, wearing her scarf and her biggest smile.

"Whoa! What's this?" her uncle said, frowning at the screen.

Minnie leaned in to get a closer look. Her uncle pointed to a comment inside a light blue box.

CD Sharp said: What's with the STUPID scarf????? And in the box below that one, Dooboy Dingle said: Why don't you cover up your ugly face too?

Minnie read the rest of the seven comments with growing horror. How could anybody do this to Amira? Amira, who was sweet and kind. Her *friend*, Amira.

"Seen enough?" her uncle said.

Minnie felt paralyzed. All she could manage was a nod. She had seen enough. She had seen too much. She could sense her uncle waiting to hear what she thought, as he always did. But she couldn't put it into words. She felt like breaking something, hitting somebody, screaming, but all she could do was weep. She sat within the shelter of her uncle's arm and wept for Amira.

"She doesn't deserve this!" said Minnie, swiping at her face. "She didn't do anything!"

"Even if she did, what kind of way is this to deal with it? Man, I'm glad I'm not a kid these days," he said, running his hand back over his head. "The old grapevine was bad enough. This is really nasty."

Minnie's tears started up all over again. She knew how it felt to be picked on, how worthless it made her feel, how hard she tried to be invisible. "I don't know what to do," she said. "Tell me what I should do."

"First, tell her to delete those comments and be careful who she 'friends,'" he said.

"And then what?"

"Then be a real friend, I guess," her uncle said. "What do you think?"

"I don't *know!*" she cried.

He patted her knee. "You'll figure it out," he said.

Minnie got to Room 2 before anybody else. She stopped at the door before going in. Why had she hurried so? What had she meant to do? Tell Miss Marks about the unhappy parents? Wouldn't she already know? Minnie waited a minute more and then she went in.

Miss Marks was sitting at her desk, in the chair for once, staring at the back wall. Her face was pink and blotchy. Had she been crying? The bell rang. Miss Marks looked toward the door.

"Minnie!" Miss Marks shot up from her chair. She was wearing something weird. A dress. A weird dress. "Wow!" she said. "I really lost track of the time."

The other kids piled in, passing Minnie stuck in the doorway like cars around a car wreck. Amira came last. Wearing a black scarf, she hurried to her desk with her head down.

Minnie went to her desk, pretending for Miss Marks's sake that she hadn't seen a thing. She watched Miss Marks trying to smile, and then actually smiling when she made a basket with a piece of balled-up paper that had been sitting on her desk. "Two points!" she said.

Was it another of the horrible drawings? Something even worse than that? Had somebody died? Her mother? Her friend Jane?

Miss Marks stood with her back to the board. The dress she had on was the ugliest, frilliest dress Minnie had ever seen, with black polka dots and lace around the collar and sleeves, and buttons like licorice drops. Her black shoes were the kind Minnie's mother called pumps. All seven studs were gone from her ear.

Alicia clamped her hand over her mouth to keep from laughing. Miss Marks looked ridiculous, as if she were trying out for a part in a play.

"We'll begin with our writing," Miss Marks said.

They were all so quiet. Instead of the usual thumps and zips and snaps and put-upon sighs, there was just the sound of getting to work. The overhead light droned.

Minnie stared at her purple pen, which was poised and ready to write. Could she really say what she felt? Or, rather, how would she say what she felt? Down through the layers of outrage and sadness was just the one simple truth: she loved Miss Marks. Not since kindergarten had she truly loved a teacher.

Sometimes what she had learned so far in this class was sad or frightening, sometimes it was stirring and hopeful and made you love that you were a human being. Miss Marks made you believe that your own good questions could change the world, at least your one small part of it.

Minnie wrote what soon began to sound like a love letter. A love letter to Miss Marks. Reading what she had written, she quickly scribbled through it. What was she thinking? She scribbled until she was absolutely sure that not a word could be deciphered. Then she turned the page over and did the same thing on the other side.

A tall thin woman with chopped-off black hair came into the room and stood beneath the American flag with her arms crossed.

"We have a guest speaker today," said Miss Marks with a tight little smile. "Mrs. Ingram, our school board president, has come to talk with us about the dress code."

Todd Ingram squirmed in his seat. He looked miserable. How awful it must be to have your mother in the classroom. And to talk about the dreaded dress code!

"Good morning, class," said Mrs. Ingram.

A few of the nicer kids mumbled a greeting back.

She didn't stay long. Mainly what she had to give them was a list of No's. No bare midriffs or navels, no baggy pants, no hats, no T-shirts with sayings on them (her eyes went straight to Miss Marks), no skintight jeans, no flip-flops, no spaghetti straps, and no headgear. "Anyone caught wearing any of the offending items," she said, "will be made to wear an oversize orange school sweatshirt." At the second offense, parents would be called in, she said. A third offense could mean suspension.

Minnie glanced at Amira, who sat straight-backed and wide-eyed. Did "headgear" mean scarves?

"I know this is mainly a seventh- and eighth-grade concern," said Mrs. Ingram. Her lips curved up for just a second, but her eyes didn't change. "However, you children are not too young to understand the consequences of immoral behavior."

Miss Marks's eyes widened. She covered her mouth and coughed. But you could see by her eyes that she'd almost laughed.

When Mrs. Ingram was gone, Derek's hand shot up.

"Yes, Derek?"

"I don't understand," he whined. "What's a moral behaver?" He scratched his head and crossed his eyes. There was an explosion of laughter.

Miss Marks bit her lip. "Okay, okay, settle down. I know it seems a little, well, strict."

"Stupid!" said Diego from the back row. "Strictly stupid!"

"Ill-advised perhaps, but they mean it. It's for teachers as well." Miss Marks looked down at her dress. "You might have noticed."

Lily's hand went up. "Miss Marks? It doesn't mean you have to give up your fashion sense, you know."

"Well, in my case it does." Miss Marks laughed and so did the rest of the class.

"Things change," she said. "Even the rules. That's the one thing you can count on."

They worked in groups to answer the questions about the story in their literature books. The story was called "Miss French's Bad Day." It was the most boring story Minnie had ever read. Miss Marks had tried to talk it up, but Minnie could tell that her heart wasn't in it. It sure wasn't *Animal Farm*.

The bell rang. Kids began moving their chairs back into rows.

"Minnie? Can you stay for a bit?"

Minnie's heart jumped into her throat. Not again! Couldn't Miss Marks see how embarrassing it was for a kid to have to stay after?

The rest of the kids, except for Amira, headed for the door. Not one kid looked back, which meant they'd be talking about Minnie the second they hit the hall. Amira was the last to leave, giving Minnie a pat for courage.

Miss Marks sat down at Amira's desk. "Is everything all right, Minnie?"

Minnie straightened her back and pretended she was Amira. "Yes, ma'am."

"I couldn't help but notice how busy you were today scratching through your journal entry. You were very determined to cover every letter."

Minnie looked down at her hands, at the blotch of purple ink on the side of her thumb.

"I just wanted to tell you that I'm here if you need to talk about anything."

Minnie felt warm and prickly, as if she might start to cry again. Miss Marks with all her own troubles was worried about her! "It's nothing," she said.

"Nothing?"

There were too *many* things—Uncle Bill's helicopter, the ugly drawing, what Derek said, Amira's Facebook page . . .

Minnie shook her head.

"Okay." Miss Marks got up. "But, Minnie?"

Minnie looked up.

"I know that some things need to be kept in our journals, you know, privately. But other things need to be said. Out loud. Even if it means upsetting other people. Even if it's scary for us. You know?" She was still looking at Minnie, but Minnie could see that her mind had gone someplace else. She had that little wrinkle frown over the bridge of her nose.

"Okay. Can I go now?"

But Miss Marks didn't seem to hear her. "You know the worst thing about adults?" she said.

"No, ma'am."

"We dish out advice but don't follow it ourselves. Here I am asking you to speak up when I—" Her eyes cleared and she shook her head, as if she'd made some kind of decision.

"I'm sorry, Minnie. I'm going to make you late for class again." Minnie watched her go straight to the trash can and retrieve what she'd made her two points with. "I just wanted you to know that I am here for you."

Minnie wanted to ask Miss Marks how *she* was doing and why she was crying, *if* she was crying when Minnie had first come into the room. She wanted to tell Miss Marks that she was the best teacher she'd ever had and one of the best human beings she had ever known. It was all waiting to be said, but it wouldn't come out. It was stuck, like her uncle in the basement.

"I'm here for you, too, Miss Marks." Was that squeaky, nervous voice hers? Had she actually spoken?

Miss Marks beamed Minnie one of her supersmiles. "Thanks, Minnie," she said.

It was like their first day with Miss Marks. As the students came into Room 2, there she was, dressed in her cool jeans with the seven studs in her left ear. Her navy blue T-shirt said SPEAK YOUR MIND in bright pink letters.

As Minnie sat down, Miss Marks caught her eye and winked.

"Miss Marks," said Alicia, "what about the dress code? It's for teachers, too, right? That's why you were wearing that ug—that dress."

Miss Marks nodded. "Yes," she said. "It's for teachers, too."

Lily blurted. "But you're wearing jeans!"

"Are they skintight?" She turned around. Her jeans were snug but you couldn't call them skintight.

"There are words on your shirt!" said Jorge. "You can't have words!"

Miss Marks smiled. "Today before we start our writing, we're going to talk about words," she said. "About language. About the way we use words to solve the world's problems or cause them. In days to come, we're going to be reading about some very famous people who stood up for what they believed, and who changed the course of our lives because they did."

Tuan raised his hand.

"Yes, Tuan?"

"Did you get fired, miss?"

"She didn't get fired," Todd said before Miss Marks could answer. His face was red, and Minnie felt sorry for him. But at least he was speaking up.

"What happened, Miss Marks?" said one of the Marias. "What made you change your mind?"

Miss Marks smiled at Minnie. "Minnie and I had a little talk," she said. "And I got to thinking. Thinking's a dangerous thing, isn't it?" Then she laughed a little to herself and turned toward her desk.

Minnie felt warm all over. It was after talking with Minnie that Miss Marks had decided to take her own advice about being "out loud." What had Minnie said? Nothing much. But she was a really good listener, and maybe that's just what Miss Marks had needed.

Could that be what Amira needed, too? Just that? Somebody to listen?

Miss Marks opened her desk drawer and took out a piece of wrinkled paper. "Let's pay attention to the language of this letter from the administration," she said. "We'll begin with the first sentence. 'It has been determined that due to unforeseen circumstances the teaching position presently being filled will not be available in the 2013–14 academic year.'"

"What a tangle!" Miss Marks said. "I'll write that on the board." She wrote the sentence and then read it again. "Where is the subject exactly?"

A few of the kids gave it a try: "Circumstances?"

"Position?"

"It?"

"Maybe. Can you find the verb?"

"Determined!" cried Lily. "It's sort of verby, right?"

"Exactly. Someone is determining something. But who is it?"

They were all stuck.

"Okay, so we know there's got to be somebody determining something because this letter got written, and sent to me."

"Miss Marks?"

"Yes, Jorge?"

"This stuff hurts my head."

Miss Marks laughed. "It does mine, too, Jorge. It's called passive voice. Some people call it 'official language,' but I think what it is, is cheating. When you talk this way, or write this way, you're not taking responsibility for your words. Or your actions. It's dishonest." She pointed to the sentence on the board. "Who knows who's doing the determining? Nobody knows for sure. That way whoever made this decision can pass the blame on to somebody else."

"But that's not fair!" blurted Minnie before she knew it.

Miss Marks smiled. "That's exactly right, Minnie. It's not fair."

AFTER SCHOOL, AMIRA FOLLOWED MINNIE UP THE CREAKING STEPS OF THE OLD SCHOOL BUS. Minnie led her to a seat toward the back. Not the back back where Dylan and the other eighth-grade boys sat, but far enough away from Carl and Derek.

As they passed him, Derek's face didn't give him away as the one who had drawn the raghead picture. He had the same out-to-lunch look on his face that he always had.

The sky was either very dark for three o'clock or the bus windows were extra dirty. Thunder rumbled, getting closer, and a smattering of raindrops danced on the roof.

The bus smelled like rotten fruit and stinky boys. It was worse than ever, or maybe it just seemed that way today. Minnie felt like apologizing for the smells, the torn seats, and the way the bus driver hauled around corners, making the kids hang on like monkeys.

As in Amira's mother's car, the girls didn't talk. But they'd have had to yell over the noise anyway.

Half the kids, including Dylan, stood as they neared

Desert Dunes, a big apartment complex. Dylan was going to Nathan's. The bus stopped and they began shuffling up the aisle.

It happened fast, so fast that Minnie caught only a glimpse of a blue sleeve: Amira's black scarf had been pulled down over her face. With a little cry, Amira quickly righted it.

"Hey!" Minnie said.

Amira squeezed Minnie's arm. "Don't!"

But nobody had turned. Minnie's voice had been so quiet she couldn't be sure she'd spoken, and now the boys were trooping down the steps of the bus like any other day. To Minnie, it felt almost like it had that awful morning in class: as if she'd jumped up and yelled at the top of her lungs. Her heart fluttered like crazy and her stomach heaved.

She looked at Amira, who was trying hard not to cry.

What color was Dylan's jacket? Was it blue?

Dylan wouldn't do something so mean. She was sure of it. Almost sure of it.

"I'm sorry, Amira," said Minnie. "It's all my fault. We shouldn't have come on the bus."

"It's not your fault, Minnie," Amira said. "It doesn't only happen on the bus."

"It doesn't?"

Amira shook her head.

"Couldn't you just stop wearing the scarf? I mean, for now. If you can. If it's not—"

Amira shook her head again. "That would mean giving up," she said. "Then another girl would give up, and another."

"But you're the only one at our school."

"I stand for all the others," said Amira, setting her lips in a determined line. She smiled a little, as if she'd embarrassed herself. "I can be stubborn sometimes."

"I admire that," said Minnie. "I admire you for doing that, for standing up for all the others."

Now Amira's smile was wide. "We are a mutual admiration society," she said.

They got off the bus at Minnie's stop. Amira popped open a huge black umbrella and held it over both their heads. "It's my father's," she said. "I don't have one of my own."

"Doesn't your father need it?" Minnie had been wondering about the father Amira never talked about.

"My father went back to Iraq," said Amira. "He didn't like America. He said Americans hate Muslims."

"Oh," said Minnie, who couldn't think what else to say.

The rain fell in heavy drops onto the umbrella.

"I haven't told you about my uncle Bill," said Minnie as they turned the corner onto her street. "He's kind of—well, he's sort of *different*. He lives downstairs in the basement. You don't have to meet him if you don't want to."

Amira looked surprised. "Why wouldn't I want to?"

Minnie shrugged. "Some people probably wouldn't. Anyway, you'll have to meet my dad and my brother. You've already met my mother."

"Yes," said Amira. "She's very pretty, and very nice."

"Yeah, she's pretty," said Minnie grudgingly. "But she's—I don't know—so *annoying*!"

"It's our age," said Amira, like a wise older person, Oprah or Phil. "Adolescent girls and their mothers get on each other's nerves. I read about it on the Internet."

Minnie's heart thumped. "You're not still on Facebook, are you?"

Amira gave her a sharp look. "Why?"

Minnie looked away. "No reason. I just wondered."

Amira stopped. Clutching the handle of the umbrella, she turned to face Minnie. "You saw my page, didn't you?"

Minnie bit her lip and nodded.

Amira's eyes turned sad. "I didn't do the privacy settings," she said. "I only wanted to make some friends."

In the shelter of the shared umbrella, rain dripping all around, Minnie wanted to tell Amira that she had a true friend now, not just a computer one.

"It was a really nice picture of you," she said instead.

"My father took that picture on the day we flew to America," said Amira. "I was so excited about coming here."

Did Amira hate America now? Minnie couldn't ask. She told herself that it was probably better not to know. "You can delete those rotten comments," she said.

At Minnie's door, Amira closed her umbrella and shook the rain off. They went inside.

Minnie's father had fallen asleep in his recliner with a stack of student papers on his lap. He was making little wheezing noises that weren't exactly snores, but were funny just the same. His reading glasses dangled from his right ear.

Minnie started to giggle, then Amira did, too. They ran down the hall and into Minnie's room, where they collapsed on the bed and laughed until they were breathless.

Minnie had worried about what Amira would think of her room, small and cluttered with everything she'd brought from her old home. She knew her American Girl dolls with their round, bright eyes and cheery faces were childish, and she wished she'd hidden Buster Bear, who looked at them from across the bed with his one good eye. But it was hard to give up the things she'd always known. Her room here in Mojave was as much like her old room as she could make it.

Minnie's mother knocked on the door. Minnie knew it was her mother because her father was asleep and Dylan would have barged right in without knocking. She thought about not answering, but knew she had to. "You may come in," she said, princess to queen.

"How about some hot cocoa, girls?" said her mother. "You can take some down to your uncle Bill, Minnie. He's probably freezing down there."

"It's not exactly freezing, Mother," said Minnie. "But okay."

Her mother got the strangest expression on her face, as if something had gone awry.

So she had never called her mom "Mother" before. Was that really so shocking?

"Well!" said her mother. "Okay then. Hot cocoa it is." She went toward the kitchen, leaving Minnie's door ajar.

"I guess it's time to meet my uncle Bill," said Minnie. She'd caught herself about to say "my crazy uncle Bill" and was instantly ashamed.

"Your dolls are very beautiful," said Amira. She lifted Samantha from the shelf. "Do you still play dolls?"

"No!" cried Minnie. "They're just for, you know, decoration. I *used* to play with them when I was little. Now I'm into, you know"—she waved her hand in the air—"other stuff."

She hoped Amira wouldn't ask about the other stuff because Minnie wouldn't have known what to answer. Since the move, she had begun to think of herself as a different person. The trouble was, she didn't exactly know that person yet.

Without Becky and Katya her life had changed almost overnight. With them, she had always known what to think and wear and do, whom to like and not like. Now she had to make all the decisions by herself, and some of those decisions—like the one to jump up and yell at the class—were totally wrong.

And she had begun to wonder if some of the decisions that her friends, especially Becky, made were right. What would Becky and Katya have to say about Amira? Could Amira have been their friend? Minnie didn't know, or maybe she just didn't want to think about it.

She led Amira into the kitchen, where her mother was pouring cocoa into three mugs. Minnie took one for herself and one for her uncle. Her mother opened the basement door, and Minnie and Amira started cautiously down the stairs balancing their cups to keep the cocoa from spilling.

Minnie was halfway down when she heard Amira shriek. She whipped around as Amira dropped her cup, turned, and ran back upstairs. Her cup rolled off the step and crashed onto the concrete floor.

"Amira?"

Minnie hurried down the remaining steps and handed her uncle the two mugs.

He had come hopping on his one leg across the room. "What's wrong?" he said.

"I don't know!" Minnie raced up the steps. There was Amira sobbing into Minnie's mother's shoulder.

"What happened?" cried Minnie. "Amira? What's wrong?"

"It's the helicopter," said her mother in a quiet voice. "I guess she thought it was real."

Shock hit Minnie like a cold ocean wave. "Oh, no! I didn't even think about that! I'm so sorry, Amira."

Amira asked for a tissue and Minnie ran to get some. Worrying about what Amira might think about her room, she hadn't even thought to mention the almost life-size attack helicopter in her basement. Minnie wanted to kick herself for being so brain-dead.

She came back with a box of tissues and Amira wiped her eyes. Then she blew her nose so delicately that Minnie wondered how she got anything out of it. "I'm sorry," she said. "I broke your cup."

Then Minnie's uncle Bill was standing in the doorway. He looked at Amira with her swollen face and black scarf, and his eyes filled with tears. "Oh, God," he said. "What am I doing?" He shook his head. "I'm sorry," he said to Amira. "I am so sorry."

Minnie started to cry. Her uncle wasn't just apologizing to Amira, but Amira couldn't know that. Maybe even Minnie's mother and her father, who had just come into the kitchen, didn't know that. But Minnie knew what he meant. He was apologizing for all the people he had killed. People like Amira.

Her uncle turned. They listened to the heavy thump of his foot as he went back down the stairs into the basement.

FROM THE FRONT DOOR, MINNIE WATCHED AMIRA WALK OUT TO HER MOTHER'S CAR. The rain was falling hard now but Amira hadn't opened her umbrella. She slid inside the car like a small dark shadow.

Minnie went halfway down the walk and stood in the rain, waiting for Amira to wave goodbye. But she didn't.

The day had been a sorry mess, the rain coming down in buckets and everybody apologizing for something. Even her mother had told Amira before she left that she was sorry.

Sorry, sorry, sorry. What good did an apology do? It made the apologizer feel better, that's all. Sometimes. And it didn't change anything.

Minnie went back into the house, tracking muddy water across the floor, for which she was not one bit sorry. She stood at the closed door to the basement and felt like kicking it. Dylan was right, their uncle was a nutcase, and now her friendship with Amira, as fragile as the cup that went rolling off the steps, was broken.

Minnie jumped as her mother came up from behind and put her arms around her. At first, angry with everybody and everything, she started to pull away. But then the tears came and she felt herself melting. She turned and sobbed, as Amira had, against her mother's shoulder.

"Were you going downstairs?" her mother said.

Minnie shook her head. She grabbed a wad of tissue and blew her nose.

Her mother smoothed Minnie's hair behind her ear. Minnie shook it free. "Your uncle feels dreadful about this," her mother said.

"Dylan's right," cried Minnie. "Uncle Bill is a nutcase!"

"Oh, Minnie," said her mother, her face drawn in disappointment.

"Well, he is!" said Minnie, stomping off to her room.

Samantha with her smug, cheery little face was sitting on the shelf where Amira had put her, only now she was leaning sideways onto Molly, who had lost her glasses. The dolls had once been able to comfort Minnie. She knew exactly who each of them was, and they never changed. Now they were just a bunch of stuffed toys. It was time to give the dolls away. She would send them to Sara, Katya's little sister.

When was the right time to give up dolls anyway? And was that a good question? Miss Marks would probably think so.

Minnie opened her journal. There across the bottom of her last entry was Miss Marks's scrawl and *three* exclamation points: "Nice job, Minnie!!!"

Smiling, Minnie smoothed her hand over a blank page and wrote down her new question.

She had written nearly a page of thoughts when the knock came.

Why wouldn't people just leave her alone? She needed a sign on her door, like Dylan had. She put down her pen and sighed, loudly. "What?" she said.

The door opened. To Minnie's surprise, there stood her uncle. "May I come in?"

"Okay," said Minnie.

Her uncle crossed to the bed and sat on the edge of her mattress. He looked down at his loosely clasped hands, then up at Minnie. His T-shirt was the color of moldy cheese. The sleeves had been torn off. The tattoo on his arm had a mean-looking eagle on it and US NAVY written underneath.

"What can I do?" he said. The rain was beating so hard against Minnie's window that she could barely hear him. The storm was gathering force.

Minnie shrugged. "I dunno."

"I could take off," he said. "That's what I should do." He smiled crookedly. "Move on with my life, like your dad says."

Minnie rubbed at the scar on her knee, which she'd gotten from falling off Dylan's skateboard. She could feel her uncle waiting for her to answer what wasn't a real question.

After a while, she heard him get up. She heard the door open. She heard him say, "I'm sorry, Minnie."

Sorry, sorry, sorry.

The door closed quietly and he was gone.

Minnie sat rubbing at her scar, remembering how Dylan had helped her up off the sidewalk and let her hold his arm as she limped into the house. Dylan used to be her hero, like her uncle used to be her hero. Why couldn't people stay the same? Why couldn't they be all good or all bad so that you knew what to expect from them?

She could almost hear Miss Marks encouraging her to write her questions down before she forgot them.

WHERE DID MISS MARKS GET ALL HER GREAT T-SHIRTS? Today's was bloodred. DON'T TOLERATE INTOLERANCE it said in wavy black letters.

Miss Marks smiled and picked up her journal. "You don't have your journals out," she said, as if she were surprised. "You don't have to wait for me to start. As soon as you come in, you can start writing." She winked. "That way you get extra time!"

"Oh boy!" said Diego. "Extra time!"

The class laughed. The journals came out, and one by one, they began to write.

Coming into the room, Minnie had purposely not looked at Amira. She wouldn't have been able to stand it if Amira snubbed her. She kept her eyes on her journal page and tried to remember her questions from yesterday, the ones that came to her after Uncle Bill had left her room.

She couldn't get out of her mind the image of his face and the look of misery in his eyes.

She wrote: "If a person kills somebody, can they ever be a good person again?"

She stared at her question until it blurred. Miss Marks was wrong about finding your own answers. There were just some things that nobody had the answer to. Minnie could write a whole book and still not know.

Which made her very uneasy. If there were no definite, final, absolute answers to a question like this, then you had to decide the answer yourself. Weren't sixth-graders too young to be asking such huge questions? Shouldn't an adult, like a parent or a teacher, be giving you the answers? Wasn't that what teaching was all about?

But Miss Marks didn't want to give them all the answers. She wanted them to learn how to come up with their own. She wanted them to help "advance the civilization," a job so big that everybody had to participate.

As Minnie began to unravel the knot of her own question, she wrote and she wrote, and when Miss Marks called time, she was still writing.

"Who wants to share?" said Miss Marks.

Minnie's heart, as always, began to thud. She thought about what it might feel like to read what she had written, and shoved that thought right down into the basement where it belonged.

A few kids shared. Then Theresa raised her hand and Minnie wanted to plug her ears again. She was definitely not in the mood for any more dead kittens.

But Theresa surprised her. By the looks on their faces, she surprised everyone, even Miss Marks.

With her head down and her hair spilling over her journal, Theresa read a story about a little girl who everybody threw rocks at because she didn't have white skin. They called her the N word, the word Minnie could hardly think, much less say. When Theresa said it, the air seemed to get sucked out of the room. Minnie was relieved that there weren't any black kids in the class. Then she realized there weren't any in any of her classes. Why was that?

Another good question.

Theresa's journal entry had ended with a question: "What if we were all exactly the same? Wouldn't that be boring?" She lifted her face and her hair fell back. Her lips twitched a tiny bit and she almost smiled.

The class applause was like a clap of thunder. They hadn't even waited for Miss Marks to start.

"Excellent question," said Miss Marks. "Now, if there aren't any more volunteers, I'd like to read an entry one of your classmates wrote and I photocopied."

After the first three words, Minnie knew it was hers,

her entry about prejudice. Her breath caught and stuck in her throat. She leaned forward so that her hair, which she wished was as long as Theresa's, fell across her cheeks. It was happening, the thing she had dreaded from the day Miss Marks gave them their new journals.

But something even more surprising was happening, too, as surprising as her behavior on the day the sub didn't show: she was calm. She listened to the words she had written and felt proud. It wasn't that the words were big or smart; they were ordinary. The good thing, the really good thing, was that the feeling behind them had gotten onto the page.

Miss Marks finished reading and smiled. To Minnie's relief, she did not look her way. "Now that's what I call thinking," she said. "Did you hear how this gir—this *writer*—didn't jump right into an answer? An off-the-top-of-the-head answer? This writer is not afraid to ask hard questions. Not afraid to hold off the answers until she—I mean, the *writer*—has thought a question through. Let's give her—um, the *writer*—some applause for a job well done."

The class clapped. Not like they'd clapped for Theresa, but Theresa didn't have the person next to her reach across and squeeze her arm.

Minnie looked over at Amira, whose eyes were shining with admiration. She felt as if her head might explode, shooting confetti and streamers all over the room. Her grin and the blush on her cheeks were giving her away, and for once, she didn't care.

With Todd's help, Miss Marks began passing out copies of a book called *Number the Stars* by Lois Lowry.

Tuan raised his hand. "Is this one all right, miss, or am I going to have to read it all tonight?"

Miss Marks laughed. "Mrs. Brennan is the one who suggested it," she said. "And it's a wonderful book. If you liked *The Diary of Anne Frank*, you'll like this one as well."

"Whose diary?" said Derek.

"Every time you open your mouth, you show how stupid you are," said Alicia.

"Alicia," warned Miss Marks.

"Sorry," said Alicia. She waited for Miss Marks to continue.

Miss Marks waited.

Alicia turned to Derek. "I'm sorry, Derek," she said. "That was a stupid thing to say."

"It's okay," said Derek with a shrug. "I know I'm stupid."

"Whoa!" said Miss Marks. "Here's a word we need to

think about." She went to the board and wrote "STU-PID" in capital letters. "What exactly is 'stupid'?"

Answers popped up around the room: "dumb," "unintelligent," "my sister," "brainless," "ignorant." Miss Marks wrote everything but "my sister" on the board. She circled "ignorant." "How about this one?" she said. "If a person is ignorant, is that a bad thing?"

No one seemed to know for sure. Then Tuan said, "Everybody is ignorant, except maybe Einstein. But he got lost crossing the street. I am ignorant about things like American history. I think 'ignorant' just means uneducated."

You could always tell when teachers really liked what a kid said because their eyes lit up. "So if someone were to call us stupid or ignorant, we wouldn't feel bad. Right?" said Miss Marks.

"Yes, we would!" yelled half the class.

"So let's cross 'stupid' out," said Miss Marks, drawing an X over the word, "and maybe it will just go away."

"Tell my father that," said Carl. "He thinks stupid is my middle name."

A few kids laughed, but only sort of.

"I think you're beginning to understand a little more about why I believe in the power of words," said Miss

Marks. "They can hurt like stones"—she looked over at Theresa—"or they can make us strong. That's why it's so important to choose them carefully, even the ones we use to describe ourselves." She looked straight at Derek. "Words have the power to change us, and to change our world."

The speaker crackled and Mr. Butovsky came on. "Please remind your parents that an open school board meeting will be held on Thursday at the county building at seven p.m. That is all."

"Who's holding it?" said Derek with a big grin, and everybody laughed.

The bell rang. Minnie waited for Amira, who was always last to leave.

As they passed Miss Marks, she gave Minnie a big smile and winked. *Nice work,* she mouthed.

"It's okay," said Minnie. "Amira knows I wrote it."

"She's a fine writer. Isn't she, Miss Marks?" said Amira.

"That's exactly right," said Miss Marks. " 'Fine' is the exact right word."

After Dylan finally came out of the bathroom, Minnie went in and closed the door. She reached in her pocket for the scarf she had found in her mother's drawer. It was a hideous scarf, but all her mother's scarves were hideous. This one had wide green, blue, and orange stripes.

Shaking the wrinkles out, she folded the scarf into a triangle and put it over her head. Frowning into the mirror, she tied it beneath her chin. Then she burst out laughing. She did not look interesting or mysterious like Amira. With her round face, she looked like one of the roly-poly peasant women she saw once on the History Channel.

She untied the scarf and stuffed it back into the pocket of her jeans. After school, if she beat her mother home, she'd smuggle it back into the drawer.

It had been a good idea. At least she *thought* it was a good idea. But she just couldn't do it.

In the kitchen, Dylan's skateboard lay upside down on the table. He was oiling the wheels.

"Uh, excuse me?" said Minnie, her fists on her hips.

Dylan looked up, then back down at the wheels.

Stupid, she thought. *Stupid.* She tried to cross the word out of her mind, but it wouldn't disappear. It was just too right for her brother.

"What happened yesterday?" he said.

"Yesterday when?"

"You know. When I was at Nathan's."

Minnie tried to decide how much of the story he needed to hear, or if he really wanted to hear it. She gave him the short version.

"I bet she got bombed in the war, or her family got bombed or something," said Dylan. He flipped the skateboard over and dropped it on the floor.

"I know," said Minnie. "What a terrible thing!"

"It's bogus," said Dylan. "War is bogus."

Minnie pulled out a chair and dropped into it. "You were right about Uncle Bill," she said. "He is crazy."

In Minnie's mind, Miss Marks said, "Crazy? What's 'crazy'?"

"No, he's not," said Dylan. "He has PTSD. That's different."

"But you were the one who said—" She gave up. "What's PTSD?"

"Post-traumatic stress disorder," said Dylan. "It's like a war hangover or something. Flashbacks. Stuff like that. When the thunder got really loud last night?"

"Yeah?"

"I went downstairs to see how he was doing. He was all hunched up in the corner and shaking like there were bombs going off."

Dylan had gone down to see how their uncle was? *Dylan?* While she sat in her room sending hate vibes down through the floor. "What did you do?"

Dylan shrugged. "Nothing. I just hung with him. You know, until the storm passed and he wasn't so scared anymore."

Minnie stared through the window of the bus, trying to sort things out. Behind her was the brother whom she'd thought of as a total jerk; in front of her was Derek, a boy she had decided was an even bigger jerk.

But it was her brother, not Minnie herself, who had gone to comfort their uncle.

And Derek? What did she really know about him anyway, except that he called himself "stupid"? He drew pictures in class. So did Theresa and Todd. Some of the other kids probably did, too. But right away she had blamed Derek. She had jumped right to a conclusion without thinking at all.

But didn't the "easy thing" prove that Derek was guilty? How would anybody have known about Miss Marks and her friend—who was probably Jane Austen—unless they'd peeked through her window?

Maybe she'd be a detective someday instead of a writer. Sleuthing was bound to be more exciting than sitting at a computer and typing all day.

She got all the way to homeroom before realizing that she had already decided Miss Marks was gay. *Whoa!* she said to herself. *Whoa!* She was as bad as the person who made the drawing.

Well, maybe not *that* bad. At least she was learning to catch herself when she made some of her stupid decisions.

Ignorant decisions.

One thing was for sure: being a person would be a lot easier if you didn't have to think.

But then what?

Last night she'd read *Number the Stars* until she couldn't keep her eyes open any longer. If Lois, the author, let Ellen, Annemarie's Jewish friend, get killed by the Nazis, Minnie was going to have to write her a letter. She was going to have to tell Lois not to kill people in her books, especially not kids. Even if it did happen in real life, you didn't have to keep thinking about it.

Unless she wrote the book so that people *would* keep thinking about it.

When her dad came in to say good night and asked what she was reading, he'd said there were people who actually believed that the Holocaust never happened. Six million people had been killed for their beliefs, he said, or because the Nazis decided there was something "wrong" with them. He said remembering that it happened might keep it from happening again.

By holding her book under the desktop in her health class and tilting it toward the inch of light coming from under the blind, Minnie almost finished the story. While the voice in the film about hygiene droned on, Minnie was standing on a balcony in Copenhagen, Denmark, watching the celebration parade below. The war had ended. She (as Annemarie) decided to wear her friend Ellen's Star of David necklace until Ellen returned.

Minnie closed the book and bit her lip to hold back her tears. Reaching into her pocket, she pulled her mother's scarf out and quickly, before she could talk herself out of it, tied the scarf on.

The bell rang just as the film ended. Minnie hurried

out of the room and down the hall without looking at anyone. She could feel eyes crawling all over her like flies. Somebody yelled, "Hey, bozo!" But she didn't know if they were yelling at her, and she didn't turn around.

At the door to Room 2, she took a deep breath and went in.

The second she saw Minnie, Miss Marks's blue eyes opened wide. Her mouth opened, too, as if she were about to speak. Then it closed and she smiled her gentle smile. She understood what Minnie was trying to do. Of course she did. Miss Marks understood everything.

Faces blurred as Minnie hurried past them to her seat: Alicia with both hands over her mouth, Lily grinning like a jack-o'-lantern, Carl frowning, Derek with his Derek look, Amira with her shining eyes.

"Before we start writing," said Miss Marks, "I need to tell you that one of your classmates, Todd Ingram, will not be with us anymore."

"Ohmygod!" cried Lily. "Is he dead?"

Miss Marks frowned. "No, Lily, Todd is not dead. He is very much alive at a military boarding school in Colorado."

All the kids began talking at once. Minnie leaned

toward Amira. "Do you think he was the one who drew the pictures?"

"What pictures?" said Amira, frowning.

"I m-mean the picture," Minnie stammered. "The one of Miss Marks."

"Let's get writing," said Miss Marks. The kids took out their journals and the buzz in the room died away.

Minnie's hand shook as she tried to write. She felt like pulling off the gross-looking scarf that she'd tied too tightly and was now cutting off her air. She'd made her point. She could slip it off while no one was watching and stuff it back into her pocket.

Why did she think the scarf was such a good idea anyway? She'd gotten caught up in Lois's book, that's all.

But it was more than that, and Minnie knew it. She was sure that Amira did, too.

She loosened the knot but kept the scarf on. She began to write.

"Time," Miss Marks said. "Who's up for sharing? Let's hear from somebody who hasn't read yet."

Minnie would have chosen to die rather than read what she'd written about how it felt today to be wearing the scarf. She kept her head down and her eyes on the closed cover of her journal.

She heard Miss Marks say, "Yes, Amira," and her heart did a flip.

In a soft, almost breathless voice Amira began to read. "This is my question," she said. "Is my father right? Do Americans hate Muslims?"

Not since Theresa said the N word had the room gone so silent. "The other day while I was riding on the school bus with my friend, Minnie," Amira read, "my scarf was pulled down over my face. What I meant to write just now is that *somebody* pulled my scarf down. It didn't just happen. Somebody did it. This same thing has happened to me three times since coming to America. On the Facebook page I used to have, people said some very mean things to me. Not because I am a girl they do not like, but because I am a Muslim. They don't even know who I am. Do these things mean that my father is right? I know that he can't be right about all Americans."

While the class applauded, Minnie thought about the raghead picture. The toilet was the exact right place for it. On top of everything else, Amira didn't need to see that.

In detective mode, Minnie glanced around the room,

searching for a guilty face. Either nobody felt guilty or everybody did. She couldn't tell. Whoever drew the picture was really good at putting on what her father called a "poker face." He or she wasn't giving anything away.

"Groups of four," Miss Marks said. "I want you to come up with at least ten good questions you have about *Number the Stars.*"

Desks scraped the floor as students moved to form groups. The kids on either side of Minnie and Amira turned their backs to make theirs.

With her hands on her hips, Miss Marks frowned at Minnie and Amira in their group of two. "Carl! Alicia! Over here."

Alicia, who was already deep in conversation with Lily, twisted around in her seat and scowled. "Me?" she said.

Carl came stomping over, dragging his desk behind him.

They all sat with their arms crossed. Then Alicia pulled an emery board out of her purse and began filing her nails.

Carl frowned at Minnie. "Why are you wearing that thing on your head?"

"It's called a scarf," said Minnie.

"Whatever," said Carl. "Why are you wearing it?"

"Did you finish reading the book?"

Carl's chin went out. "Did *you*?"

Minnie nodded.

"The whole thing?"

"Yes, the whole thing," said Minnie. "If you read the book and you still don't know why I'm wearing this, I'll tell you."

"We should start our list of questions," said Amira. "I'll record them."

Filing away at her fingernails, Alicia said, "Question number one. Why do we have to read this stupid book?"

"It's not stupid!" said Minnie. "It's a great book. It's all about prejudice and hate and what can happen if we don't stop it!"

Alicia rolled her eyes.

Amira wrote down Alicia's question, leaving out the word "stupid." "It's a legitimate question," she said.

Carl, who hadn't even started the book, was no help. He drew a picture of a "rad" snake tattoo he was going to get on his bicep.

Minnie thought he was going to have to wait to do that since he didn't have a bicep yet, or at least not one you could see.

Alicia, who had read up to page fourteen while watching *Glee*, didn't have any questions to add.

Minnie and Amira came up with the remaining nine questions while Carl drew and Alicia filed. But when Miss Marks asked each group to write their best question on the board, Alicia hopped right up. "Why do we have to read this stupid book?" she wrote, straight across the top of the board in huge red letters.

Miss Marks shook her head and sighed. The bell rang and everybody headed for the door.

"I think they're going to fire Miss Marks," said Amira once they were in the hall.

Minnie stopped in her tracks. "Who?" Kids streamed around them like fish, some going upstream, some going down.

"I don't know," said Amira. "I heard my mother talking to one of the other parents on the phone. They're all going to the school board meeting to complain about Miss Marks."

"But she's the best teacher I ever had!" cried Minnie.

"Yes. Me, too."

"What can we do?"

Amira shook her head sadly. "I don't know," she said. "Go to the meeting, I guess."

Minnie felt a tug on her neck as the scarf went down over her face. When she pulled it back, she saw the same thing had happened to Amira.

They looked at each other for a minute, and then they cracked up. They laughed all the way to art class.

Minnie took her painting to a table. She had given it a title. *Marin: A Girl with Questions.* Question marks in a rainbow of colors surrounded Marin's head. There were thought bubbles, large and small, filled with questions. Maybe someday she would paint on a face, but for now her self-portrait was finished.

A WHITE PICKUP TRUCK WAS PARKED AT THE CURB IN FRONT OF MISS KELLER'S HOUSE. LEWIS & SONS WINDOW WASHING said the sign on the side. A man in white overalls got out on the driver's side. A teenage boy got out on the other side. The back door opened. A younger boy got out and grabbed a bucket and rags from the bed of the truck.

It was Derek.

Minnie stopped in the middle of the walkway to her house, replaying what Derek had said that day on the bus. Was the "easy" thing washing Miss Marks's windows?

Minnie's hand flew to her mouth. How could she have gotten it all so wrong?

And what about the drawing? Had she gotten that wrong, too?

"Mom? Dad?"

Both cars were in the driveway, but her parents were gone.

Dylan came in as Minnie was searching the house. "Where are the folks?"

"I don't know. Maybe they went for a walk."

"Mom? She parks in the handicap spaces so she doesn't have to walk so far to the store."

"She does not!"

"Okay, so she doesn't. Got your attention though!" He punched Minnie's arm and Minnie socked him back. "Ooooooo, you're hurting me!" he whined.

"Mom? Dad?"

"Down here," came her father's voice.

Minnie and Dylan locked eyes. Uncle Bill was in trouble.

They went down to the basement, where their parents and uncle were drinking coffee and talking. Nobody looked upset, so Minnie let out her breath.

Her uncle smiled at her, smiled as if she'd done nothing wrong, as if she hadn't let him down. She felt terrible.

He patted the sofa cushions on either side of him. "Take a load off, kids."

"So," said their father, as if they'd broken for a commercial and were back on the air, "all we want to know—and we think it's fair to ask—is why, Bill."

Their uncle scratched the back of his neck. Frowning,

he nodded for a while to himself. Then he looked up at their father. "Why am I building an attack helicopter? I thought I knew. Now? Now I don't know. I haven't figured out what I needed to know."

"Which was?" their father said.

"Why it went down. Why I lost this leg. Why my buddy lost his life."

"Oh, Bill," said their mother, her eyes filling with tears.

"We were flying low. It was dark. We had Night Sensor, Target Acquisition Designation, the whole nine yards. Pete had the gunsights locked on a suspicious-looking truck. We saw some men get out of it, Iraqis. Hijabs, turbans. They were holding what looked like a rocket launcher.

"I took the chopper lower. We were counting down when I spotted two kids climbing out of the back of the truck. I remember yelling 'Abort!' "

He rubbed his face hard, like he was washing off dirt.

"Then, I don't know, I must have jerked the stick, hit a power line. *Something*. Because we went down."

Minnie could see by the look in her uncle's eyes that he had gone back to where it all happened. She laid her head against his arm.

"If it weren't for that Iraqi family, I'd be dead, too," he said. Tears rolled down his cheeks into his whiskers.

"I came in and out of consciousness in the back of that truck, engine whining as they pushed the old wreck as fast as it would go toward a hospital. Every time I woke up, I felt a small hand in each of mine. Their eyes—" He turned to Minnie. "Like Amira's," he said. "Like your friend's eyes." He frowned. "The rocket launcher? A rolled-up canopy, the kind they use in their open-air markets."

Nobody said anything for a while. The sink drip-drip-dripped. Their uncle looked at their mother for permission before lighting up a cigarette. Leaning back against the sofa cushion, he blew a long plume of smoke into the ceiling. "I know it sounds irrational, but I thought that by putting myself back into that chopper and thinking, *thinking*, what could possibly have gone wrong . . ."

He flicked ashes into his coffee cup. "I know there were problems with the BUC system, but that was in the older models. And swashplate failures in some of the tail rotors." He shrugged. "But that's hard to duplicate in a model." He leaned back and the air seemed to go out of him. "I haven't wanted to believe that it was pilot error," he said. "But it could have been. It could have been."

Their father was as quiet and still as Minnie had ever seen him be. "You've got to let it go, Bill," he said. "You can't let it run your life."

Their uncle's laugh wasn't a real one. "Tell me about it," he said.

"Thank you for sharing this with us, Bill," their mother said. "We didn't understand."

"I'm sorry it took so long for me to tell you," he said.

Minnie stayed behind with her uncle when the others went upstairs. He sat with his head against the cushion and his eyes closed. There were dark circles under his eyes. She wondered if he slept at all, or if he just wandered around town all night with his hands stuffed in his pockets and his head down, thinking, thinking.

"I'm sorry," she whispered.

"What for?" he said.

"For being so mad at you. For not coming down here when you were scared in the storm."

He smiled, his eyes still closed. "I wasn't scared," he said. "I was terrified."

He opened his eyes. "Don't be so hard on yourself, Minnie girl. You've been my best friend for months."

"You've been *my* best friend," she said.

Minnie knew when he said "So what's going on with your new teacher?" that he was doing his best to shake off his sadness.

Miss Marks didn't feel new to Minnie anymore. She

felt as if she had known her teacher forever. "They want to fire her," she said.

"Who wants to fire her?"

"Some of the parents," said Minnie. "There's an open school board meeting tonight to talk about her."

"Hot time in the old town tonight," her uncle said.

"Huh?"

"It's an old song."

"Will you come?" said Minnie.

"To the meeting?" He frowned, then he clapped her on the thigh and made her jump. "Sure," he said. "For you, Minnie? Anything."

"Silver clogs?"

"Silver what?"

"Clogs," she said. "Shoes."

"You want me to buy you a pair of shoes?"

"You said anything."

"You little manipulator! Okay, tonight the meeting. Saturday next week when my check comes, we'll go buy you some clogs."

"You mean it?"

"Yeah," he said, his lips in a grim line. "I mean it. Where better to re-enter the world than at a shopping mall?"

MINNIE SAT BETWEEN DYLAN AND UNCLE BILL IN THE BACKSEAT, NERVOUSLY TAPPING HER FOOT. She wondered if Miss Marks would be at the meeting. If she was allowed to be at the meeting.

They couldn't keep her out, could they? Didn't "open" mean everybody?

She hoped that Amira was already there and that she'd saved some seats. Minnie's mother had taken forever to "refresh" her makeup, and they were almost late.

"What's that?" said her father as they neared the county building.

Minnie leaned over the seat to look through the windshield. Up ahead were a bunch of people yelling and waving signs. HONK IF YOU LOVE MISS MARKS! MISS MARKS IS THE GREATEST! RETAIN MISS MARKS!

"Well!" said Minnie's mother. "I didn't know she was so well-liked."

Dylan hooted. "I guess you're running with the wrong crowd, Ma!"

Their mother sniffed. "Their opinions are not necessarily mine," she said.

On the next corner were more signs. FIRE MARKS! MARKS NOT OUR KIND! SHOW HER THE DOOR! COMMITTEE OF CONCERNED PARENTS.

"Oh, dear," said their mother.

Their father parked the car. "Let's go on in," he said. "Get a seat in the front."

But when they got inside, the only seats left were in the back. The boardroom was packed. Some people had brought their signs inside but had to put them down so that everyone could see.

A table and six chairs sat on a raised platform. Six microphones and six bottles of water were spaced evenly along the table. There were signs that said each board member's name. Ten past seven and they hadn't yet come in. The room, already warm, was getting stuffy. People were talking, laughing quietly.

"I'll bet they didn't expect this crowd!" said the man sitting next to Minnie's father.

Minnie was thrilled. No way could they fire Miss Marks now!

A tall, very thin, very white man came in behind

a short woman with orange hair and a deep tan. "Mr. Hamisch" and "Mrs. Johnson" said their signs. They were not smiling. Next came three women who looked like sisters because of their identical hairstyles: Mrs. Rose, Mrs. Peters, and Miss Winkler. Miss Winkler smiled, but only a little. Then she began fidgeting with some paper in front of her.

Mrs. Ingram came in last and sat down behind the sign that said "President Ingram." With a bang of her gavel, she called the meeting to order and everybody stood to say the Pledge.

"There are a number of items on our agenda," Mrs. Ingram said when they were seated again. She picked up a piece of paper and scanned it. "We need to finalize the budget. That should take the bulk of our meeting time. Then there are the two items tabled at the last meeting."

She looked up as if she were seeing the audience for the first time. "Then there's the matter of . . . Lindsay Marks, who's currently on leave. Is that right?"

On leave? Miss Marks was on leave? When did that happen? After school. It had to have been after school or she would have told them.

Three rows in front of Minnie's family, a woman

popped up so fast her black hair bounced. "Marks is teaching our sixth- and seventh-graders." She smirked when she said the word "teaching." "A teacher like that belongs in a . . . in a zoo!"

"But she's doing a great job!" said a man in the front. "And I don't know about your kids, but my kids aren't monkeys!"

Cheers went up in several places like popcorn.

Mrs. Ingram's gavel came banging down. "Everyone will get a chance to speak," she said. "In the meantime, we'll have no out-of-order comments or you'll all be dismissed."

It was like a big foot had been planted squarely in the middle of the room. No one said a word.

Minnie's mother whispered, "I'll bet she was a teacher once."

"Or a judge," whispered Minnie's father.

The board started in on the budget, using words like "shortfall" and "certificated personnel." Minnie noticed that nobody ever said "we" or "our." Instead, they said things like "it has been decided," and "before that issue is tabled again." It was hard to know from what they said who was doing the deciding or the tabling, but of course everybody had a pretty good idea. They were using official language. Nobody could blame them for making a bad decision because decisions had simply "been made."

Minnie's heart sank for Miss Marks. "It has been decided," Mrs. Ingram would say, and Minnie would never see Miss Marks again.

She craned her neck to try to find Amira but didn't see her.

The agenda went on forever. Minnie laid her head against her uncle's arm and closed her eyes. Time passed like she was at the dentist's office.

". . . Lindsay Marks."

Minnie's eyes popped open and she sat straight up.

"The floor is now available to members of the community who wish to speak to this issue," Mrs. Ingram said. "If you'll come up and take the mic one at a time, please."

A microphone was handed to a woman who marched up from the second row. "I am a concerned parent, and there's a chance that my daughter will be in this teacher's class next year if she's not fired. And I'll tell you right now, I will have no part of her brand of teaching! All that dark, depressing stuff! I want her gone, and now!"

As if this were a classroom, there were hisses and boos from the back of the room, and the woman sat down.

A man stood and said that his daughter was in Miss Marks's class and that she was reading now instead of watching television. "That's one good teacher, if you ask me," he said.

A woman with red frizzy hair stood up, bouncing on her toes as she talked. "What about the high-stakes tests? What about No Child Left Behind? My Lily hasn't done one practice test in Miss Marks's class! I don't want my child left behind!"

"They waste too much time writing!" said another parent. "Isn't it supposed to be an English class?"

Some people laughed.

Mrs. Ingram's sharp black eyes scanned the room. "That's it? Well, I've got something to say. I'm speaking as a parent now. I know this is irregular, but I have a stake in this issue. My son was in Miss Marks's class." She crossed her arms. "And there's a chance my daughter will get her if she's here next year. For the record, I'd like to mention just a few of the things that went on in my son's class."

Todd was a snitch! Todd the helper. Todd the model student. He was only pretending to like Miss Marks. Was this the reason for his hateful self-portrait?

"First, all those questions!" said Mrs. Ingram. "With

no guidelines for what might be inappropriate! They could ask about"—her face turned red—"elephant farts! They could write about viciousness and dead cats. She even said the N word. In class!"

Minnie jumped up, her heart pounding and her head about to burst. "She did not! She didn't!"

"Sit down, young lady," said Mrs. Ingram, pointing her gavel. "I am not finished."

Minnie sat down. Her uncle put his hand on her shoulder. "She's lying," Minnie said.

"Her students have not spent one class period practicing for the standardized tests. Not one. Instead, they read about pigs and communism and Nazis! They draw ugly pictures in their notebooks! She's indoctrinating them to accept the gay lifestyle."

Minnie was on her feet again. "Stop!" she cried. "That's not true!"

"Sit!" said Mrs. Ingram, as if Minnie were her dog.

Then Minnie's father stood. "Excuse me," he said in his lawyer voice. "Things are getting a little out of hand here. You're making charges based on nothing more than the word of one child in Miss Marks's class who happens to be your own son. That's slander. I suggest that you watch what you say."

"I beg your pardon!" said Mrs. Ingram as the blood drained out of her face.

Minnie's father continued. "To my knowledge, school boards have no authority to deal with personnel issues. But, since this is an open meeting, my daughter, Minnie, has the right to speak."

The board members on either side of Mrs. Ingram leaned in to advise her.

"Very well," she said. "She may come up and take the microphone when I have finished." She cleared her throat and took a sip of water. "Some of you might not know that Mojave Middle School has a mandated dress code that Miss Marks—a teacher!—has broken nearly every day that she has stepped onto the campus. Clearly her message to our young people is to defy authority. Get a tattoo! Punch holes in your ears!"

Laughter bubbled through the aisles.

Mrs. Ingram pointed at the audience. "You may think it's funny now, but marks my word—I mean, mark my words—" She threw up her hands. "Okay, that's it. Let Mary come up."

"Minnie," said Minnie's father.

Minnie's uncle pushed a little on her shoulder. "Go on," he said.

WHEN MINNIE STOOD FOR THE THIRD TIME, HER KNEES TURNED TO WATER. Somehow she made her way down the row without falling into the aisle.

People turned in their seats to see who was coming. Some were smiling, some frowning. *A child? What did a child have to do with all this?* There were whispers. Somebody coughed. Somebody laughed.

Minnie caught a glimpse of Mrs. Ingram's narrow, angry eyes. Dizzy, she walked to the front of the room and reached for the microphone.

Turning to the audience, she said in a shaky voice, "My name is Minnie McClary." The microphone shrieked and she nearly dropped it. She held it away from her mouth. She took a deep breath. "I am in Miss Marks's sixth-grade language arts class."

The room grew quiet, as quiet as snowfall on the day she'd learned to ski at Mammoth Lakes. All morning long she had fallen down, bruising her knees and elbows, while Dylan whizzed past on his snowboard. But she hadn't given up. She hadn't chickened out. Some things were superhard, but you just had to do them.

Being short actually helped when it came to skiing, but not when it came to giving speeches. She asked for something to stand on.

A man in the first row brought her his chair. Holding the microphone, she climbed up. There was Amira in the very back row, looking terrified. Minnie's mouth felt dry, her tongue was like a big, fat sponge. The chair was rickety, the microphone heavy in her hands.

She cleared her throat. "I just want to say that Miss Marks is the best teacher I have ever had."

People's smiles seemed to be saying, "Oh, isn't she cute?" as if Minnie really had nothing to say. Her ears began to burn. "Maybe you think that because I am only a sixth-grader I don't know what good teaching is, but I do. And so does every kid in my class." Her voice cracked. She turned and asked for some water.

Miss Winkler handed Minnie her water. Minnie's hand shook as she opened the bottle and tipped it to her lips. Then she went on. "I know that passing the state tests is important, but they're never about what we're studying. Do you know that? They just get in the way of the good stuff we're reading."

Some people frowned, others nodded. "Anyway," said Minnie, "I don't need a teacher to help me fill in bubbles, I need a teacher who helps me feel smart. And that's what Miss Marks does. She encourages us to think and to ask really important questions. She says that someday we will be making all the big decisions about what goes on in our world and she wants us to be ready."

People seemed to be listening seriously, and Minnie could look at some of the faces, even the ones who weren't smiling.

"Well," she said, feeling a little like Miss Marks, or the way she thought Miss Marks must feel standing in front of the class, "how can we learn how to be leaders if we don't know how to ask the right questions? If everybody just pretended to know everything, our world would be in big trouble."

More nods than frowns this time, and Minnie forged on. "Not one grownup has come into our classroom to watch Miss Marks teach. If they did, they would see what a great teacher she is. So, like Tuan, a boy in my class, says: 'There's something else going on.'"

People sat straighter in their seats. Some leaned a little forward. Minnie had piqued their interest. What was the "something else"?

"Miss Marks doesn't dress like the other teachers. She dresses young." Minnie bit her lip. "I mean, the other teachers aren't, like, *old* . . ."

Now they were laughing. Minnie had lost them. She took a deep breath and collected herself.

"Here's what I think is going on," she said, as if she had a fat, juicy secret. The audience settled to hear what it was. "Here's why some people want to fire Miss Marks. Last Wednesday, Miss Marks wore a T-shirt that said 'Live out loud' on it. That's why she's in trouble, because of things like that, like what she wears and what she believes. And maybe because of what some people think she is, and that's not fair."

Minnie's mouth had run completely dry, but her mind had not. She took a sip of water. "People are jumping to conclusions about Miss Marks without thinking, without knowing what really goes on in our class. That is prejudice and it's just plain wrong."

The loud burst of applause startled Minnie. People were on their feet. Her father, mother, uncle, and brother were clapping like crazy.

"Yay, Minnie!" cried Amira, punching the air in a very un-Amira-like way.

Minnie turned and looked right at the scowling

school board president. "Instead of firing Miss Marks, you should be looking for more excellent teachers just like her." She handed the microphone back. "That's all I have to say."

Shakily, she climbed down off the chair. Her face in flames but her head held high, she walked all the way back down the aisle to her seat.

THEY ALL KNEW THEY'D BE HAVING A SUBSTITUTE LONG BEFORE THEY GOT TO CLASS. They always did. Nobody knew the whereabouts of Miss Marks, but that didn't stop the rumors from flying: Miss Marks was gone forever, the police had taken her out in handcuffs, wearing an orange Mojave Mustang shirt that came down to her knees; Miss Marks was terminally ill, her mother was terminally ill, her grandmother died, her girlfriend died.

Minnie refused to listen to any of it. Miss Marks would be back. She would not leave without a fight. And she would not leave forever without saying goodbye.

The sub was one they'd never seen in any class before. He had no hair and no eyebrows, but he did have a big barking voice. On each of their desks was an official-looking booklet.

"I am Captain Roger Davis, United States Army Retired. My hearing and eyesight are perfect and I don't take prisoners. Open your test-prep booklets and read the introduction."

Wide-eyed, Alicia leaned across the aisle and whispered to Carl, "What's that supposed to mean?"

"It means he kills people," Carl said. "It's an Army thing."

"What is your name, young lady?" Captain Davis said. His pointing finger came within an inch of Alicia's forehead.

"Um, Alicia. I'm sorry! I'm sorry I talked, I won't do it again."

Captain Davis wrote "Alicia" in the right-hand corner of the board in red block letters.

"And your name?" he said to Carl.

"Do you really kill people?" said Carl.

"Do I what?"

"What you said about prisoners."

"Ha!" If the captain had eyebrows, they would have gone up. "That's for me to know and for you to find out."

Lily raised her hand. "Is Miss Marks coming back?"

"I wasn't told," said Captain Davis. "But I will be here for the duration."

The class erupted. "How long is that?"

"What's a duration?"

"Did she get fired?"

"Is she ever coming back?"

"Are we going to do journals?"

"Are you a real language arts teacher?"

There were food spots on the front of Captain Davis's plaid shirt and a little tear in the pocket. For some reason, this made Minnie feel sorry for him. She always felt sorry for subs. If they tried to be nice, they were destroyed in the first ten minutes. The mean ones took a little longer.

The first stealth plane hit the captain square in the middle of his forehead. His face turned beet red and his voice climbed one whole octave. "Okay! Who threw that? You! You in the back row! What's your name?"

"Bart Simpson."

While the Captain wrote "Bart Simpson" on the board, a whole fleet bombed him. It was an endless fifty minutes, with kids taking turns humming the same monotonous note until Captain Davis was banging the language arts book on the desk and yelling for order.

Minnie opened her journal and read the letter to Miss Marks that she had finally written, just in case the worst thing happened and Miss Marks never came back.

It was a pretty good letter but it would never get sent. First, because she didn't have Miss Marks's address. Second, because it was way too personal and embarrassing, and third, because Miss Marks would be coming back, she *would*.

At dinner that night, Minnie begged her father to find out what had happened to Miss Marks. He said he didn't think substitute teachers had any rights under the law, but that he would look into it.

Captain Davis was there again on Monday, and the day after that. He drilled and drilled them on parts of speech and vocabulary until even he looked bored and weary.

Nobody seemed to know whether Miss Marks would be coming back soon or next year, or would ever come back at all. No rumors seeped through the halls. It was as if Miss Marks had never been.

Minnie raised her hand on the fourth day, as if she'd always done it, as easy as that. "Captain Davis? Do you know anything at all about Miss Marks?"

"Well," he said, scratching the back of his neck, "I know she's in Florida."

Lily squealed, "Florida!"

"Then she's fired?" said Diego.

"Is she coming back?" said Jorge.

"What about the stupid school board?" said Derek. They all looked at Todd's empty seat.

"It's not up to the school board," said Minnie. "It's up to the superintendent. And they're not stupid, they're—"

"Ignorant!" yelled the class.

"Calm down, calm down," Captain Davis said. He held up both hands like a traffic cop. "I know you all like Miss Marks, but I really don't know any more than you do."

"Will you tell us when you do?" said Minnie.

Things got very quiet then. Minnie, somehow, had said the perfect thing. Whether or not Captain Davis would ever be one of them depended on his answer to her question.

"Yes," he said, and gave a little nod of confirmation. "I will."

"Cool!" said Carl, and for the rest of the period, no matter what Captain Davis said or did, it was okay.

Well, almost okay. He talked too much about weapons of war, and he was tougher on the boys than he was on the girls. But he was their ally now.

The next day, Captain Davis took an envelope out of his briefcase. "In my box this morning I found this letter.

It's addressed to you." He held up the envelope so they could see the slanted writing. Then he turned it around to show that it hadn't been opened.

"Open it!" cried Alicia.

"Read us the letter!"

"What does it say?"

"To My Fourth-Period Sixth-Graders," Captain Davis read. "I'm sorry that I left without saying goodbye. I was told to turn in my keys and not to return to the school until further notice."

The class groaned.

"This made me very sad. You will be growing and learning so much the rest of this year, and I would love to be there with you. It was my great pleasure to be your teacher for as long as I could be. But the class goes on. Please remember that. Without you, there is no class. Be the students I know you can be, not only for the rest of the year but for the rest of your lives. Ask questions and expect answers. Speak up for what you believe, and care for others the way you care for yourselves. I will never forget any of you. With love, Lindsay Marks."

Captain Davis folded the letter and put it back in its envelope. "I have some good news," he said. "At least for me it is. I will be your new long-term sub."

He smiled like a kid who'd gotten socks instead of toys for Christmas, a sad, good-boy smile. Nobody cheered. They were still sunk in their sadness over losing Miss Marks. Some of the girls, including Minnie and Amira, wept.

"She sent some photos," said the captain. "I'll just put them on the—"

Everyone rushed the bulletin board.

"Let me see!"

"Let me see!"

Amira pulled Minnie through the taller kids to the front.

There were five photographs. One was of Miss Marks standing under a palm tree in front of a building with three balconies. It didn't look fancy, but the tree was nice. "My mother's condo," she'd written on the back. Another showed her at the beach. "Gross ugly swimsuit!" said Alicia. "She should get a bikini. She's got the body for it."

"I'm sure she'd appreciate your advice," said Captain Davis, shaking his head in dismay. "You can write to her, you kids. Stand back while I tack these up. I need to breathe."

The next photo was taken in front of an IHOP. "My temp job," she'd written on the back.

"Won't she be a teacher anymore?" said Lily.

Captain Davis stapled the corners of the IHOP photo. "Oh, I'm sure she will be," he said. "Teachers never retire. They just lose their class. Ha-ha."

"Is that a joke?" said Tuan.

In the fourth photo, Miss Marks was standing with a chubby, dark-haired lady wearing a ton of gold chains. "My cool mom," she wrote.

In the last photo, Miss Marks was standing on a rock in what looked like a big park. She was wearing her LIVE OUT LOUD T-shirt and flexing her biceps. There was nothing written on the back because there didn't need to be. They all knew what she was telling them.

"You go, girl!" said Lily.

Captain Davis went back to his desk. "If you'll all come and sit down," he said, "I'll give you the rest of the period to write Miss Marks so we can mail your letters in one big envelope this afternoon."

Minnie took out her journal and reread the letter she'd already written. It was a good letter. Kind of mushy, but it came from her heart.

She hoped Miss Marks knew that she had stood up for her at the school board meeting. It wasn't a thing she could tell her, and it didn't really matter. What mattered was that she had done it.

Dear Miss Marks,
(This is my homework letter. I'm sorry it's so late.)
My name is Marin Elizabeth McClary, but everybody calls me Minnie. This is fine, except that I'm so short. On my first day at this school, I heard somebody call me "Minnie Winnie," and then somebody else whinnied. So either I'm a travel trailer or a horse.

I am new to Mojave Middle, and maybe that's the way it is here, but I don't think it should be. At my old school in Pasadena, the kids all learn about teasing and bullying and how bad it is for the kids on the receiving end. I was never on the receiving end until this year.

I guess it sounds like I'm feeling sorry for myself, but I'm not really. When I think about what happened to you and to another girl in our class, who doesn't want me to whistle-blow, I know it can be so much worse.

Whistle-blowing is what got us to Mojave in the first place. I have three heroes in my life right now. The first is my dad, who did the right thing and lost his job because of it. The second is my uncle Bill, a real live war hero, who lost his leg fighting in Iraq. He has a purple heart and a bronze star.

The third hero in my life right now is you, Miss Marks. At first (please don't feel bad about this) when I saw you wearing your faded jeans and sitting on the teacher desk, I didn't think you were a real teacher. Now I know what a real teacher is. Like Jorge said, you make our brains hurt, but in a good way.

I don't think that I will ever be an artist, but I'm thinking very hard about becoming a writer and telling people what I think. It's very hard to do it in person, so I figure writing is the next best thing. Or maybe the best thing, I'm not sure yet.

I pray every day that you will return to our school. I'm sure God knows what a good teacher is and will send you back to us. If He doesn't, He will hear from me. Big-time.

Yours truly,
Minnie McClary
Period 4, 1st row, 4th seat
Mojave Middle School

Minnie folded her letter and slipped it into the manila envelope when it came around.

"Miss Marks left me a letter, too," said Captain Davis, his bald head shining like he'd polished it. "She wrote down all the names of the troublemakers, so don't think you'll be getting away with anything."

They all turned to look at each other. Who was this guy? Miss Marks would never do a thing like that.

"Okay," he said, with his big hands on his hips. "So she didn't tell me. But she said you had to write in journals, so don't think you're going to get away with not doing that!"

The whole class cheered.

Captain Davis shook his head. "You *want* to write?"

He got nods from almost everybody. "Okay, then," he said. "Do it."

They all took out their journals and wrote until Carl, standing in for Miss Marks, called time.

IT WAS SATURDAY. Minnie, twisted all up in her pj's, had been trying to sleep in when the house started falling apart.

That's how it sounded anyway.

Rubbing her eyes, she went into the kitchen, where her mother was reading the weekly newspaper. "What's all that noise?"

"See for yourself," said her mother.

Minnie opened the basement door. "Uncle Bill?"

Halfway down the steps she saw what was happening: her father and uncle were taking apart the helicopter, piece by piece.

The heat was thick in the basement and both fans whirred furiously. Her father and uncle were covered with sweat. The helicopter listed to one side like a giant bug injured in a sci-fi movie. Minnie almost felt sorry for it.

Had her uncle given up trying to find out what brought the chopper down?

As the banging and tearing continued, Minnie went back upstairs. What would her uncle do now that he didn't have the chopper to work on? Would he sleep away his whole life?

Minnie took a pound of bacon out of the fridge and laid as many slices in the big frying pan as it would hold.

"I'm going to take a shower," she said.

Her mother, caught up in the newspaper, said nothing.

"Mom? I said I'm going to take a shower."

Her mother would catch on when the bacon started to sizzle. It was a nice trick to get her to make breakfast.

Something was bothering Minnie, like a gnat that wouldn't stay out of her face. She turned the shower full on and stepped in. Water battered her head and woke up her brain.

She knew what it was then, the thing that kept bugging her. She had given up. Standing up for what she believed in had been thrilling, and for a little while she had felt victorious. Powerful. Huge. Four-foot-six-inch Minnie McClary had wowed the crowd. But now it was over.

Was that it? Was that what she was missing? Feeling like a star? Was it just a selfish thing after all?

She cranked off the shower and grabbed a towel from

the rack. Ugh. If you slept in, this was what you got: a damp towel. It matched her mood perfectly.

She dressed in a ratty pair of cutoffs and a dark blue T-shirt that said nothing at all.

She stomped into the kitchen. "Don't forget that I'm going to Amira's ballet lesson today," she said.

"Oh, my gosh!" her mother said, not at the bacon that was spitting grease all over the stove, but to something she had read in the paper. "Look at this." She laid the paper on the table and pointed to a small article at the bottom of the Features page.

Sub Teacher's Job on the Line

by Joshua Bernstein, Features Editor

Take it from a reporter who has covered far too many interminably boring school board meetings: this one was anything but. The fate of Lindsay Marks, a young teacher hired as a long-term substitute at Mojave Middle School, rests in the hands of Superintendent Brian Dawson: will she return to the school and the students clamoring for her, or will she be terminated and another long-term substitute be hired to take her place?

Minnie McClary, one of Miss Marks's avid sixth-grade language arts students, wants her teacher back.

"She's in trouble because of . . . what she wears and what she believes," said Miss McClary, standing on a chair and clutching the microphone. "And maybe because of what some people think she is, and that's not fair."

I wasn't the only one to stand up and applaud. If Miss Marks's teaching helps produce students like Minnie McClary, I'm with her: bring the teacher back.

Her face warm and her heart pounding, Minnie read the article twice.

"Well, how about that, Miss Minnie McClary?" said her mother. "Get me the scissors. You can save this in your scrapbook."

"What scrapbook?"

Her mother frowned as if Minnie had a booger hanging from her nose. "You don't have a scrapbook?"

"Nope," said Minnie. "Should I?"

For once, her mother didn't have an opinion. "Well, I don't know," she said. "I had one at your age."

"But I'm not you," said Minnie.

"No, you're not," her mother said. "I never would have stood on that chair and talked to all those people."

"But you were a cheerleader!" said Minnie.

Her mother smiled as if she could still see the pom-poms. "When I was sixteen," she said, "and part of a squad. Nope, you got your courage from your dad, not from me."

Minnie snagged a piece of bacon. "Do you think Dad will ever be a lawyer again?"

"I don't know, honey. He got very interested in teacher rights after that meeting, I know that. And he has an appointment with the superintendent this afternoon."

"Oh, Mom!" cried Minnie. "Do you think he can get Miss Marks back?"

"Maybe she doesn't want to come back," said her mother, lifting an eyebrow. "Did you consider that?"

"She does!" cried Minnie. "I know she does! How can you even think that?"

Minnie stomped out of the kitchen. What was the matter with her mother? Didn't she know *anything*?

After school, Minnie watched Amira going through her ballet exercises at the barre. Amira's long dark hair was in a bun, and she was wearing a black leotard. When she stretched an arm into the air, her back was ruler straight.

Minnie was sure that Amira had grown at least an inch since the start of school. If ballet lessons could do that for a person, Minnie was going to start taking them.

It was either that or stand on chairs for the rest of her life.

Or clogs. She couldn't wait to go to the mall with her uncle this afternoon. Silver clogs! Could anything in the world be better than silver clogs? She deserved them, didn't she? After what she had done?

And there was that nagging thought again. Why had she gone up and given her little speech? Was it only to defend Miss Marks?

"So what do you think?" said Amira, pulling off her ballet slippers, her forehead shiny with sweat. "Would you like to take lessons?"

"Maybe," said Minnie, but her thoughts had returned to where they had been earlier. "Amira?"

Amira wiped her face. "Yes?"

"The other night when I, you know, stood up and said all that stuff about Miss Marks . . ."

"Yes!" said Amira, clapping her hands to her chest. "You were great! You were like a . . . like a rock star!" Amira laughed. "Sort of. You know, fabulous!"

Minnie frowned. "That's just the thing," she said. "It all feels so weird now. Like I was doing it for, I don't know . . . to get famous or something."

"Oh, no!" cried Amira. "That's so not you, Minnie.

You were scared to death. I thought you might faint and fall off the chair. Your face was completely white."

"It was? Did I look dumb?"

"Dumb? No! Brave! You looked very scared and very brave. I was so proud to be your friend." When Amira pulled out the scrunchy, her hair fell softly to her shoulders. She whipped a maroon scarf over her head and tied it.

"You're brave, too," said Minnie.

"We should start a club," said Amira. "Or, I don't know, do something."

"A mutual admiration club?" said Minnie, remembering what Amira had said that day on the bus.

Amira bit her lip, thinking. "No," she said. "Something else. Something bigger."

It happened like it happens in cartoons. Minnie felt a light go on over her head. "I know," she said. "We need to make a stand."

"A stand? Like a lemonade stand?"

"Nope. A people stand," said Minnie.

MINNIE SLIPPED HER RIGHT FOOT, THEN HER LEFT FOOT INTO THE SHINY SILVER CLOGS. She knew exactly how Cinderella must have felt.

Her uncle (the prince) slouched in the seat beside her with his arms crossed and a big grin on his face. "So that's what you want?" he said.

Minnie nodded vigorously. She clomped across Macy's tile floor and back.

Her uncle frowned and shook his head. "Little girls," he said.

"I'm not a little girl!" said Minnie hotly.

He looked at Minnie very seriously. "No," he said. "You're not. You're not little at all. It all happened so fast, you took me by surprise, that's all."

"*What* happened?"

"You grew up."

"It's the clogs," said Minnie. "I'm two inches taller."

"It's not the clogs, Minnie," said her uncle. "It's you."

"Why did you join the Navy?" said Minnie, the clog box with her old Skechers inside tucked under her arm. She set the box on the kitchen table and followed her uncle down the basement steps.

What she saw there made her catch her breath. She closed her eyes, not wanting to know what the basement was telling her: her uncle was moving out. His moth-eaten blanket lay folded neatly on the sofa, three boxes had been packed with what she guessed were his clothes. His laptop was in its case, the library books he'd borrowed in a neat stack waiting to be returned.

Minnie burst into tears. Her uncle put his arms around her. "It's time, Minnie," he said. "Like your dad says, I've got to get on with my life."

"Why didn't you tell me?" Minnie sobbed.

"I didn't know," he said. "I wasn't sure until last night. I've been afraid, Minnie. Afraid that I'd end up like so many vets out there. On the street, broke, homeless. Scared to look people in the eye. Scared to take a risk, go back to school, find a new life."

"Can't you stay here and do all that?"

He shook his head. "You know how I hop around here sometimes without my prosthesis?"

Minnie nodded.

He looked down at his "good" leg. "It's to let this one know it can go it alone," he said.

"Do Mom and Dad know you're leaving?"

"Not yet. We'll tell them together, how's that?" he said. "But first I've got something for you." He opened a small box and took out a bronze star dangling from a red, white, and blue ribbon. He pinned it on Minnie's T-shirt. "It's for Meritorious Achievement in Ground Operations Against a Hostile Force," he said. "I think you qualify."

Minnie laughed. "For real?"

"Well, the Navy wouldn't say so but I do."

Minnie put her hand over the medal. "I'll keep it for you," she said. "Not forever, because it's really yours. Just for a while, okay?"

"It doesn't match your clogs," he said. "Guess I should have gotten the silver star, huh?"

"Oh, Uncle Bill," said Minnie. "Matching is, like, so *yesterday*."

"Who knew?" said her uncle.

They went in the old Volvo to the airport, where her uncle bought a one-way ticket to San Francisco. "You don't have to hang around," he told the family. "My plane doesn't leave for a couple of hours."

"We'll wait," said Minnie's father in his don't-argue voice.

They wandered around the shops, where her uncle offered to buy Minnie and Dylan anything they wanted. Minnie, over her mother's objections, got a copy of *Teen People*. Dylan got a duffel bag with a Dallas Cowboys logo and six giant-size Snickers bars.

At last it was time for their uncle to go. Minnie followed him all the way to Security, as far as she was allowed.

"You never told me why," she said.

"Why what?"

"Why you joined the Navy in the first place."

The skin around her uncle's eyes crinkled, ready to smile or frown. "I don't know, Minnie. I love this country. And I guess . . . I guess I wanted to be a hero. Part of me, a big part of me," he said, "did it for the glory." He shook his head, his eyes growing dark. "We do things for lots of reasons, Minnie. Mostly to feel good about ourselves, worthwhile. I don't know. I wanted to change things, make the world safer." He laughed a little. "But I was the one who got changed."

"I love you, Uncle Bill," said Minnie, grabbing her uncle around the neck, easier to do now that she was two inches taller.

"I love you, too, Minnie girl," he said. "I'll e-mail as soon as I land somewhere."

Minnie watched him go through the scanner, his back as straight as any soldier's. He turned to wave, joined the crowd heading for the gates, and was gone.

"I'm scared," whispered Amira.

"Me, too," said Minnie. "We look ridiculous. We aren't even a line. If we didn't have these signs, nobody would know what it is we're trying to do!"

STAND AGAINST HATE said the sign that was beginning to feel very heavy. They had made it the night before, choosing black paint instead of a brighter, happier color like orange or red. "Hate" dripped a little, which, they decided, was a nice touch.

Amira's sign said JOIN US in bright red letters. At their feet were several other STAND AGAINST HATE signs for the other kids they hoped would join them.

But nobody did. Kids hurried past, glancing quickly at the signs and pretending not to see them. Or they stopped, which was way worse, and said all the awful things Minnie had expected, and a few she hadn't.

"Hey, stupids! Get a life!" said an older boy walking with a pack of his friends.

"What are the scarves for?" said another. "To hang yourself?"

Minnie's face felt stiff, as if she were wearing a mask. Amira was on the verge of tears, but when she lifted her head, the bright butterflies on her scarf lifted, too, as if they might fly. Minnie had chosen to wear the brightest scarf in her mother's drawer. Red, white, and blue zigzags with bright yellow stars.

She was beginning to learn this about herself: when she decided to do something, she did it big.

The bell would be ringing in thirteen minutes and classes would begin. Minnie's right arm ached from holding up her sign. The glare of the sun made her squint. Why hadn't she thought to wear sunglasses? The big black, bug-eyed ones her mother had worn before she got her "designer shades." She could hide behind them and the kids wouldn't know who she was.

She sighed. Thirteen minutes could feel like thirteen years.

They saw her before they knew who she was, a slim blonde coming out of the faculty parking lot, wearing jeans and a green T-shirt, a backpack slung over one shoulder.

"Miss Marks!" cried Minnie. Dropping her sign, she

took off running. Both girls tackled the teacher they thought they'd never see again, almost knocking her down.

"You're back!" cried Amira.

"Yup," said Miss Marks, smiling her biggest smile. Her seven—eight!—studs glittered in the sunshine. Her toenails were the color of broccoli. Her shirt said CELEBRATE in sparkly gold letters. "I'm back and I'm bad!"

"You're not bad, Miss Marks!" said Amira, missing the joke. "You're good. You're the best teacher in the world!"

"No, I'm not," said Miss Marks. "But I'm all yours. At least until the end of this year."

Minnie and Amira threaded their arms through their teacher's and walked beside her.

"What's this?" said Miss Marks, stopping to look at the signs scattered on the lawn.

"We're taking a stand," explained Minnie. "My grandma stood in a line with the students at her college to protest the Vietnam War. She said it worked."

Miss Marks picked up one of the STAND AGAINST HATE signs. "This is an even bigger war," she said. "We'd better get started." She turned to face the kids rushing by and held up the sign. Minnie and Amira held up theirs. The three of them stood together in their little line.

"Miss Marks?" said Alicia, wide-eyed. She and Lily had come to a screeching halt in front of them.

"Join us," said Miss Marks, her smile as welcoming as ever.

Alicia and Lily looked at each other. They looked to their left and right, at other kids, seventh- and eighth-graders. Kids who might laugh at them.

"Uh, no thanks," said Alicia.

"It's a good idea though," said Lily as they hurried away. "A really good idea!"

"We'll be here tomorrow!" said Minnie.

"And the day after that!" said Amira.

"For as long as it takes," said Miss Marks.

Three boys on skateboards whizzed by. They all stopped, but only one came walking back.

Dylan flipped back his hair. "What's going on, Minnie?"

Of all times to start playing big brother! "What does it look like, Dylan? We're taking a stand against hate."

When Dylan frowned and nodded, Minnie could see his resemblance to Uncle Bill. It made her smile.

"Hate is bogus," said Dylan. Flipping up his board, he stepped into the line and stood beside Minnie.

And then two girls stepped in, looking scared and holding hands.

It was a line. Not a long line, not yet. But it was a beginning.

Then Minnie saw Derek. He was standing a ways off, watching them. "Come join us, Derek!" she said.

To her great surprise, Derek, with his Derek look and his shuffling walk, did just what she said. Nudging a place between Minnie and Miss Marks, he got into the line.

And Minnie, who didn't feel at all like a hero or a rock star but a little like somebody who maybe, just might be making a difference, stood straight and tall in her silver clogs, her smile as bright as the desert sun.

ACKNOWLEDGMENTS

Love and gratitude to Frances Foster, my editor and the "midwife" for my books since 2002. There is no one like Frances, as everyone who has ever worked with her knows. Along her way, Minnie McClary was very fortunate to be in the capable hands of Susan Dobinick, Frances's assistant, and grew up with the invaluable help of Gwen Dandrige, Kim Hernandez, Sherrie Petersen, and Lori Walker. My thanks to Raine Nelson-Grua for making me at least appear Facebook savvy and to my always-first editor and love, Jack Hobbs.